SALVATION

N GRAY

By N Gray

Blaire Thorne

Ulysses Exposed

Voodoo Priest

Butterflies and Hurricanes

Salvation

Underworld Legacy

Scout Thorne

The Secret Tomb

Murder of Crows

Shifter Days, Vampire Nights, & Demons in Between

Twisted

Lady Hawk and Her Mountain Man

Hidden Shifter

Wolf

Wolf Retreat

Night Hunter

The Fixer

Kai

Lee

Flynn

Jude

This is for you!

Vinci Books

vinci-books.com

Published by Vinci Books Ltd in 2025

1

Copyright © N Gray 2020

The author has asserted their moral right to be identified as the author of this work in accordance with the Copyright, Designs and Patents Act 1988.
This work is a work of fiction. Names, characters, places and incidents are the product of the author's imagination or are used fictitiously. Any resemblance to actual persons, living or dead, places and incidents is entirely coincidental.
All rights reserved. No part of this publication may be copied, reproduced, distributed, stored in any retrieval system, or transmitted in any form or by any means, including photocopying, recording, or other electronic or mechanical methods, nor used as a source for any form of machine learning including AI datasets, without the prior written permission of the publisher.
The publisher and the author have made every effort to obtain permissions for any third party material used in this book and to comply with copyright law. Any queries in this respect should be brought to the attention of the publisher and any omissions will be corrected in future editions.
A CIP catalogue record for this book is available from the British Library.
Paperback ISBN: 9781036702311

The EU GPSR authorised representative is Logos Europe, 9 rue Nicolas Poussion, 17000 La Rochelle, France
contact@logoseurope.eu

Part I

10 YEARS AGO

Chapter One

I drove while Ralph leafed through documents in one of his yellow folders. I was sure he bought them in bulk, because he always had at least ten on hand. He seemed to collect them like others collected stamps. I giggled to myself imagining him hunched over his worktable, separating them by the different shades of yellow. He kept paging forward then backward then forward again, flapping loose pages then placing them back in the folder.

"What are you looking for?" I asked with irritation laced in my voice.

"I just want to make sure we have the right guy. That's all."

I sighed. "It's a vampire, Ralph. I can feel it in my bones. Now stop paging through that damn folder. You're messing with my Zen."

"Pfft, whatever!"

"We're here anyway, so shove it somewhere out of sight."

We arrived at Lake Hills Institute for Children. The

sinister-looking building was three and a half stories high; the half was for the creepy attic at the top with broken crescent windows that looked like a mouth missing some teeth. The building was once white, about a hundred years ago. Now it was grey with some areas near the ground rotting away with black mold. I wouldn't want to be near the place when it crumbled to the ground, but I felt sorry for the kids who wouldn't grow up. The only parking bays taken were cars that belonged to the medical staff, which weren't that many. I parked beside an old sun-kissed box BMW near the entrance.

A gust of wind blew through the trees, and a chime sounded from somewhere inside the institute. A cold shiver ran down my spine. I stood on one spot and stared at the trees.

"Come on, princess. I'm not getting any younger." Ralph moaned as he climbed the stairs to the entrance.

An eerie feeling washed over me. I ran my fingers over the gun in my shoulder holster. Touching the cool metal was soothing and eased my fight-or-flight instinct. Now I was ready. Well, kind of.

"Someone's out there." I rubbed my arms and headed toward him.

"You know what to do if the boogeyman jumps out of the forest?" He chuckled.

"Yeah, I'll use you as a shield as I test drive our new bullets."

Ralph continued chuckling as he ascended the steps.

"Glad I'm still amusing." I elbowed him in his side.

"Come, partner. Your favorite doc waits." He wrapped his meaty arm around my shoulders and dragged me to the front door.

I groaned as we reached the entrance. The smell of

urine assaulted my nose first, stealing my breath. I stopped breathing to avoid the stench. On the other side of the locked metal gate, a naked young boy sat on the floor busy mixing a yellow substance into the dirt that had gathered in the corner.

I widened my eyes at Ralph.

"Please, Blaire, just don't piss off the doctor again," he chastised me even before I could say anything.

"Well, well, well. Look what the cat dragged in," the nurse chimed from behind her glass cage.

"Nurse … whatever your name is, can you not see the little boy urgently needs your help?" I pointed to the dirty, naked child.

"Not my duty, monster killer." The nurse folded her arms and pursed her lips.

"It's not only monsters I kill." I glared at her then added quickly, "Is the doctor in? He's expecting us." I shot her my best fake smile.

"Wait here. Let me check." She rose from her torn chair and exited the glass cage, disappearing somewhere in the institute.

"I fucking hate this place." I felt I needed a hot bath and to scrub my skin with a body brush until I bled.

"What did I just say?" Ralph grumbled.

Shrugging, I added, "I didn't piss off the doctor."

"No, but that nurse will tell him and piss him off all the same."

"They hired us, Ralph. They should be glad we're even here."

"Let me do the talking, please." His shoulders sagged, and he gave me his best blue puppy-dog eyes.

"Fine. But only because you looked so cute when you asked, and you said the magic word." I grinned while he groaned. He hated it when I called him cute, but it's hard to resist his charm.

On the right-hand side of the entrance hung a plaque with a large picture frame. It read that the school had opened in 1889 and housed talented children. I wasn't sure if they meant the kids had some form of disability or were mystical or magical. But the kid on the floor didn't seem the latter. Twenty staff members adorned the photo, all dressed in white, comprising of nurses, orderlies, and the man in the middle who ran the place—Curtis Hilling. Underneath the frame hung more plaques stating which of the Hilling sons had taken over and from which year. Arthur took over from his father in 1901. Isaac ran the place from 1946, Charles from 1983, and, lastly, Lu from 1999.

The buzzer sounded, and the gate clicked open.

"Dr. Hilling can see you now. Go straight to his office. If you don't remember where it is, just walk down the hallway. You can't miss it. It has his name on his door, if you aren't sure. If you can't read, just look inside the office. He's sitting at his desk."

Ralph pushed open the gate.

I followed him and closed the gate behind me. I started walking toward the door where the nurse sat in her little glass safety office, but Ralph pulled me away to walk beside him. I would not do anything that hurt too much. I was just going to tell the nurse we remembered where the doctor's office was. Maybe slap her. Instead, I stared at her with murderous intent.

The smell of feces wafted in the air as we passed the boy. He was now pushing brown mushy stuff through circles of yellow mud.

I covered my mouth with both hands and gagged—yuck.

A cockroach scurried past me and met up with its buddies on the other side of the corridor. I shuddered. This place was not sanitary and should definitely not be housing any children, no matter their age. I didn't think it was safe for adults, unless a cleaning crew made the place sparkle, which I doubted. The institute had years and years of grime stuck everywhere that needed to be burned, not just cleaned. And I would gladly light the match.

As we approached the doctor's office, one side of the corridor wall displayed brown finger marks about hip high in a wavy pattern, as if the child had run dirty fingers against the wall as he or she went along. I hoped it was mud. I wasn't confident it was and wouldn't stick my tongue there to test it either.

Ralph entered the office first to find Dr. Lu Hilling sitting behind his desk, as the nurse had said. He ignored us until Ralph cleared his throat.

Dr. Hilling glanced up; for a moment he just stared as if he didn't recognize us, then eventually, he smiled, rising from his chair. "Ralph, Blaire. So good to see you again. Please, won't you come in?" He walked to a trolley and picked up a jug. "Can I offer you something to drink?"

"No, thank you, Dr. Hilling," I said, eyeing the suspicious liquid.

"I'm good," Ralph replied quickly.

I was sure he would rather lick the wall than drink what Dr. Hilling offered us in that jug.

"Are you sure?" Dr. Hilling confirmed, pouring the liquid half-way into a glass then another glass. "The water comes fresh from our well." He picked up both glasses and placed them on his table, each opposite a chair. "Please sit."

We sat, and I eyed the brown-yellow substance. Water my ass.

"Thank you for coming. Hopefully, it won't be a waste of your time again." Dr. Hilling sat in his soft, comfortable chair while we sat on hard wooden ones.

"How old is the child who went missing this time?" I asked, wanting to get straight to the reason why we were there. Again.

Ralph widened his eyes at me. Apparently, I forgot I couldn't speak to the doctor.

I shrugged.

Dr. Hilling cleared his throat. "Eight." He leaned back in his chair, threading his fingers and placing them on his large stomach.

"When was she taken?" Ralph asked.

"Sometime last night."

"Does anyone check on the kids during the night?" I asked, ignoring Ralph's fierce glare.

"Only after lights out, thereafter, once again after five hours."

"So—"

Ralph kicked my shin.

I bit my bottom lip, trying to ignore the sharp pain shooting up my shin. This was partner wars, and he just threw the first kick. I ignored him like any good partner would and continued my questioning. "All these children you look after, are they only supervised when somebody is around?"

Dr. Hilling nodded, the hair framing his face showing signs of grey. His deep-set brown eyes seeming to burn a hole into my forehead. If he had knives, I was sure he would throw them at me. He bounced upright in his chair and hit his hands on the desk, making me flinch. The yellow water rippled in the glasses.

"With the limited resources they give us, we care for

these children to the best of our abilities, Miss Thorne. Without us, where would they go? And we rely heavily on donations ever since the government stopped funding us." He rose, towering over us. Shadows played on his face, leaving him with sinister features. "Let me take you to the room from which they took her. Perhaps you can pick up on clues we may have missed."

Ralph stood. "That would be great."

Dr. Hilling exited his office with us following. The good doctor was around my height and had a round, supple ass that bounced with each step. From the front, his hair was short and neat; from the back, a tight ponytail secured the bottom half of his hair. His shoulders were as broad as mine, while his front showed signs of small round breasts where, I assumed, he would strap them close to his body.

Dr. Lu Hilling, as we had suspected the first time we had visited, was actually Louise Hilling—born female. We didn't mind what our client's sexual orientation was; the job always came first. It was, however, how he performed his job that made us suspicious.

Ralph elbowed me, I lost my footing and crashed onto the first step, knocking my shin. I was sure it would leave a bruise, especially since this was the second time I had hurt myself. I cried out in pain.

"Are you all right?" Dr. Hilling asked, bending to help me up.

I waved him away. "I'm fine, thank you. Just knocked my leg. Perhaps take Ralph up while I rest on the steps?"

"Fine. Come, Ralph."

I watched Ralph and Dr. Hilling disappear up the stairs, then I ran back to his office. I had about a minute. I rifled through the papers on his desk and opened the drawers to find invoices and folders for food orders and purchases. On the right was a metal filing cabinet I hadn't tried yet. I opened the bottom drawer first and found bank statements. What caught my attention was the wire transfers from the institute into Dr. Hilling's personal bank account.

Voices echoed down the hallway; they were on their way back. I rose from his chair and ran to the stairs as quietly as my shoes would allow. I sat on the step as I saw Ralph.

He winked.

"See anything interesting?" I asked, steadying my breath.

"Nope, but I suggested we look around outside. Last time, they cut our visit short, but today, we have all the time in the world." Ralph beamed at me as he walked past.

Dr. Hilling offered me his hand. When I grabbed it, I felt a hint of magic behind his grip; hot pinpricks fluttered across my palm.

I'd had enough practice not to show signs I held any power nor did I reveal I could register power. It's safer that way for me and anyone who knew me.

Dr. Hilling blinked, and, for the first time, I noticed a nictitating membrane; a transparent third eyelid moved across each eye, similar to that of a crocodile or lizard. He was not even human. How had I not seen that coming?

I revealed nothing as I stood and followed Dr. Hilling and Ralph outside.

"As I've said before, this isn't the first child to have gone missing, Miss Thorne. This vile monster has taken five of our precious children already."

I nodded in disgust. "We will catch them, Dr. Hilling. Whoever the monster is will pay for what they have done."

Once outside, I saw a handful of kids skipping rope, another drawing with chalk on the cement, and one girl laying under a tree. I did a double take at the girl under the tree. "Is she clothed?" I asked, shocked they would allow a young girl to be naked outside. Older men worked here. I said a silent prayer, asking that they weren't hurting any other kids.

"There are"—Dr. Hilling cleared his throat—"some who do not listen to us." He waved over an orderly. "Please arrange for Miss Bayle to be dressed, and give her Diazepam if she resists you."

"Do you medicate them often, Dr. Hilling?"

"I fail to see how your questions are relevant to the case at hand, Miss Thorne. You need to find the beast who's kidnapping my children and doing who knows what with them, not question how I run my facility."

Sucking in air and patience, I responded as calmly as I could. "I need to understand what's happening at your institute, Dr. Hilling. Maybe these children are choosing to leave your institution at their own free will, or, as you suggest, someone's stealing them from right under your nose. I only ask these questions so we know exactly what is happening here. And, if it is a monster taking the children, we need to stop them sooner rather than later."

Dr. Hilling blinked, and again, I saw that third membrane slide across each eye, and he fidgeted with his sleeve.

Ralph cleared his throat, slicing through the uncomfortable silence. "I suggest we widen our search and go farther into the forest. Is that gate always open?" He pointed to a weathered gate that had seen better days. Even if it was always locked, monsters could break it with a sneeze. Or jump over it. Some monsters could fly, no matter the size of the lock or gate.

"No. It's supposed to be locked," Dr. Hilling said, rushing in the gate's direction.

The lock was broken and laying on the ground. I guess someone sneezed after all.

"You stay here, Dr. Hilling. Ralph and I will be back. And please take all the kids inside. It's not safe for anyone to be outside until we catch this monster." I pushed passed him with Ralph behind me.

Dr. Hilling didn't answer me. Instead, he turned and ushered the kids inside like a good doctor following orders.

Chapter Two

"What?"

"Did you have to speak to him that way?"

"Yes. You saw how those kids looked, how they were treating them."

"I saw, but sometimes you don't have a filter."

"I don't care. That place doesn't help kids. They're using them. For all we know, Dr. Hilling is the one taking them and disposing their bodies. Then he blames a so-called imaginary monster."

Ralph sighed.

"He's also a reptile."

"What?"

"I saw his third eyelid."

"Shit."

"Yeah, shit. Who knows what he's doing to those kids. He could be *flesh hungry*."

"Okay, I get it. Just stop speaking in that voice." He pushed me jokingly. "Let's search out here for an hour before going back then walk around the institute again."

I nodded in agreement.

We walked deeper into the forest that surrounded the land. They had built Lake Hills Institute for Children before the were-animals, vampires, wizards, witches, fay, and all the otherworldly creatures could move around freely without the common folk hunting them down and killing them—before they became legal. The forest that is Sterling Meadow hadn't been split into the various sections yet. The were-animals still hunted in secrecy. The fay and faeries hid harder. Trolls perfected the art of being immovable boulders. Vampires lived in shadows and fed on unsuspecting victims but not killing them, as the body count would cause chaos; they merely seduced and hypnotized them. And witches pretended they were normal humans, masking themselves in their trinket shops or wagons.

My partner, Ralph, was a plain vanilla human. He had absolutely no idea of my abilities. It was safer for him that way. I'd had years of training to hide what I could do. I had a great teacher—one of the best. My ma.

Here we were again. They had offered us a job, someone was taking children from this institute and never seen again. Dr. Hilling didn't want the police or any kind of authority to discover what was happening, so he called us—Ulysses Assassins. He needed the illusion that it was still a great institute and to maintain his wealth—*ahem*, to ensure the children were properly cared for. His bank statements were proof of my suspicions. He was using the institute's donations to fund his private bank account. I informed Ralph we now had confirmation of what he was doing because of the documents I had seen when I searched Dr. Hilling's office. Now we just needed to ensure that Dr. Hilling didn't destroy the evidence by the time we notified the police.

As Ulysses Assassins, we hunted and killed mystical beings who stepped over the metaphysical line and caused chaos. And I would love to get my hands around that doctor's neck and squeeze. Every once in a while, we sorted out humans too.

But first, I had to do this. I lowered my metaphysical shield and searched for the monster who might be taking children. I felt … something, like a change in wind direction. I stepped from behind Ralph and approached an area where the trees were denser. The gold, yellow, and red leaves had already fallen to the ground.

Ralph realized I wasn't behind him any longer and followed me. After a few minutes, we reached an old shed with its weathered walls. A thin line of smoke rose from a deadened fire, and next to it was a log he or she sat on.

"Let's check the shed." I touched the handle; it was cold, obvious no magic protected the shed. I pulled the handle, and it opened slowly to a coffin laying in the center of the small room.

"How can a vampire survive out here? Can we open it and throw his ass into the sun?"

"He could be innocent."

Ralph tapped my shoulder.

I turned to look at him and followed his line of sight. Just on the outside of the little piece of land where the shed met the forest was a heap of clothing.

"Let's look here first. If a vampire is here, we need to ensure he's still sleeping."

Vampires were tricky sonsofbitches; not only could they manipulate you into doing what they commanded, but some were powerful enough to withstand the sun for short periods of time. For a vampire to be out here, unaided by any kind of magic, told me he was powerful. And it was damn suspicious being right here by the institute where children played.

"I'll open it. You stand ready," Ralph instructed with one hand on the coffin lid.

Nodding for him to go ahead, I un-holstered my gun and aimed it at the box while he opened it.

He lifted the lid at a painstakingly slow pace. Inside was a young man/vampire with flecks of blood on his shirt and a smear on his chin.

"Please, can I throw him in the sun?"

"No!" I groaned, staring at my watch. "It's almost dusk. We wait."

Ralph lowered the lid until it clicked closed.

"Why?" he whispered as he tiptoed out the shed.

"He can't hear you. He's dead to the world. And besides, I want to speak with him. There's more to this story than just a vampire camping out in a shed."

We exited the tiny vampire house.

"Let's check out the clothing." I pointed at the stack Ralph saw earlier. With a stick, I pushed the various items off the pile and onto the ground, so I could open them up. "They belong to a girl." My heart rate increased, and I wanted nothing more than to ram this stick into the vampire's heart.

"Shit. I can't look at that."

I turned to find Ralph by the fire pit, pushing a stick in the ashes. "I doubt the fire is hot enough to burn bodies out here. Plus, everyone at the institute would have smelled the body burning."

"He burned something here," Ralph added, still poking the ashes with his stick.

I crouched for a better look.

"Pages from a book," Ralph said, pushing a half-burnt page from under the ash.

I picked it up and groaned. "Three little pigs." I dropped the page and wiped the ash on my clothing. My pulse thundered in my ears. My jaw ached from clenching my teeth. "As tempting as it is to throw out his ass, we still need to ask him questions. Otherwise, we are no better than the cops."

"Yeah," Ralph said, sighing.

The cops were notorious for killing first and asking questions later. Even though we were assassins, we needed to ensure we had our man or foe. It was no use going out guns blazing and killing innocents. Although they were all guilty in my book. I had come a long way from my first kill with Marcus by my side. He was like a father to me at first. Then greed got the better of him. Now all he did was book our targets while we did the killing.

The sound of my cellphone brought me from my thoughts. I stood and glanced at the little screen with the text message. *He found us, Blaire. Help!!!*

"Shit …"

"What's wrong?" Ralph glanced in my direction with concern etched on his face.

"Nothing. But I have to go. I'm sorry." I started walking.

"You can't leave me here."

I didn't answer him when I started running. A cold sweat washed over me as I squeezed my eyes shut and ran faster, muttering every known swear word no one could hear.

Chapter Three

I'd worked so hard at not being found, yet he still found us.

I jumped into Ralph's vehicle, grabbed the keys when they fell from the visor and fired up the engine. I mashed the gas and drove into traffic, easing my foot off the pedal when a patrol vehicle pulled in front of me. I maintained the speed limit until the patrol vehicle turned left.

When Mason and I had met, I had explained my situation and about *him*—why I had to get away, and why I couldn't let him find me. He had found me once before, but Laine—the man who was to bring me to him—had protected me and paid the price with his life.

I slammed on the brakes and opened the door, but the vehicle rolled forward. I jumped back inside to pull the handbrake. Climbing out the vehicle again, I ran across the street. Mason and Scout were at our neighbor's house—Hugh and Jermaine, Scout's godfathers.

"Mason, come," I yelled as I pounded on the door.

"Hey, Blaire," Jermaine said with wide eyes as he opened the door. "You guys are scaring me."

"I'm sorry, but the less you know the better. Come, Mason!" I yelled again, more from fear than anger. My body trembled as I took Scout from Mason and held her close to my body. The feel of her warm, tiny body against mine was comforting. She pulled on my hair and filled the house with her giggles. My heart sang at the sound of her wonderful voice, but fear threatened us more, and I had to keep us all safe.

When we were back in our house, I went straight to our room, sat Scout on the bed and paced. "What happened, Mason?"

"At first, I didn't know who he was." Mason exhaled slowly. "But he walked right up to me as I left the daycare center with Scout in my arms. He said, *'She looks just like Blaire.'* When I asked him who he was, he said, *'Tell Blaire an old friend is back.'*"

He wasn't telling me everything, and he still looked spooked. "What else? You know better than to keep anything from me."

Mason glanced at Scout then at me. "That man said if he couldn't have you, he'd have Scout."

I sucked in air, tension squeezed my shoulders, and I blinked back tears. "Fuck. Did he follow you home?"

"I don't know." Mason shrugged.

"Think, Mason, think. Was someone behind you as you drove home?" My voice quivered as panic took hold of me. If they had followed Mason, then they knew where we lived. We needed to plan properly, so we were ready for them if they burst through those doors at any moment. One thing I knew was Scout couldn't be here if that happened.

I had taken Mason to the shooting range often enough, so he knew all about guns. And he came with me to practice fighting at the gym. We even reviewed what he needed to look for if he thought someone might tail him. I knew he would protect Scout with his life, but I needed to ensure nobody had followed him *here*.

"No. I didn't see anyone."

"He can't have her," I said with unshed tears. "You need to take her and hide."

"I can't leave you." He pulled me into an embrace.

"You have to. I'd hoped he would forget about me, but obviously, he hasn't. And we can't allow him to have her. Ever." My emotions were raw, and I felt vulnerable again. If anything happened to her, I would die. But not without killing as many of them as possible.

"What aren't you telling me?"

"What do you mean?" I stared at the floor.

"When we met, did you tell me everything about him?"

I couldn't look at him.

"Well?" he asked sternly.

I slumped onto the bed. "I told you after that man had killed my mom, I went to live with my aunt and grandmother."

He nodded. "That there was a bad man, your aunt's *friend*."

"Yeah, the family seemed to attract bad men. What I didn't tell you is he was a werewolf." I squeezed my eyes shut then shuddered. "He was a sadist. He frequented those clubs and turned my kindhearted aunt into a shut-in. She never left the house after meeting him and was so blinded by what he really was, she ignored all the other women he messed around with. We all could see it except her. What I didn't tell you, on my thirteenth birthday, he gave me my first kiss, as unwanted as it was. He forced my first kiss onto me, said he would wait until my flower had matured."

"Fuck." He fell onto the bed beside me, staring straight ahead at nothing to mull over my words.

"Then, when my gran died, he said he couldn't wait to be my new daddy and take me out for father/daughter dinners." I choked up at the horrid memory but refused to waste tears on him. "I had to get away before he hurt me. That's when I left my aunt a note, packed my bags and ran. She died three or four years later."

"Was it him?"

I nodded. "I used to call her every month to hear how she was doing. When she didn't answer me that last time, I knew something had happened, but I didn't want to go back. The newspaper said someone had murdered her. I just don't have the details. But I know it was him."

He gently rubbed my back. "Why didn't you tell me this?"

"I don't know. I guess I'd hoped he wouldn't find me again, and I wouldn't have to bring you into all this crap."

"Well, he has found you. What should we do?"

"You'll take Scout, change your names and disappear. I'll stay here and fight him or make him go away. I don't know yet, but I'll figure it out."

Mason flinched with a shocked expression as if I had just hit him. "No," He shook his head. "No!"

"You have to." I stood and grabbed two bags from the closet, so I could pack their clothes.

"Come with us."

"If I come with you, he'll just search for me again. He's already said if he can't have me, he'll take Scout. What will we do if he finds you and Scout on your own?" My voice raised. "He might kill you to get to her." I stepped backward, rubbing my temples with my thumbs. "We can't take the chance. We have to keep her safe."

"I know, but I can't bear the thought of leaving you here on your own." He wrapped his arms around me and kissed the nape of my neck. "I'll miss you."

I turned to face him and hugged him tightly against me. "I need the two of you to be safe while I deal with him," I said into his chest, wiping my face and smearing my tears on his shirt. I had to be strong for them. I couldn't afford to crumble now. If Mason knew how my heart was breaking, he wouldn't go, and I needed him to. I needed them both away and safe. My life meant nothing should anything happened to them. And I would do everything in my power to keep them both out of harm's way.

He kissed the top of my head then rested his chin there while we embraced. It might be our last one for a while. But my personal comfort was a small sacrifice if it meant their safety.

"How will you find us?" he finally asked, sounding like he was deep in thought.

"We can work that out later." I stepped away from him to finish packing their clothes.

An hour later, I had finished packing their bags and semi-formulated a plan. I removed a stack of cash from the safe in the floor near my bedroom window and handed it all to Mason, his mouth agape when he saw the safe and the money.

"W-what? It's like I don't even know you. When did you install that?" He jerked his chin in the safe's direction and hesitated before accepting the money as he noticed the other items in the safe.

"I'm sorry," I whispered. "I truly am. I haven't shared some things with you, but I only did it to keep you safe. Some things I cannot share with anyone."

"Some things?" He raised his voice. "What else aren't

you telling me?" He crossed his arms, his breathing quick and heavy.

I placed a calm hand on his arm, but he shrugged me away. His expression was tight, offended, and empathetic as we stared at each other. A storm of emotions crossed his face in a blink of an eye—anger, sadness, hate, fear, and tenderness. My emotions matched his, with two extras for good measure—frustration and regret. Regret for not going after *him* and killing him myself instead of waiting in fear for him to find me. But I had let down my guard. I was finally in a good space and happy. I had fallen in love, and I'd had a baby; life happened. This was my punishment for not listening to Ma. I hated karma.

"I thought he'd forget about me and move on. I didn't think I'd put you or Scout in danger." My words were soft, filled with hurt and impotent rage.

"Well, you did. And now you're forcing us to run away," he retorted. "Will I ever see you again?"

"You will, but only when it's safe to do so. Once things have settled down and he's out of our lives for good." I picked up Scout for one last embrace. "I'm sorry," I whispered into her hair. Then I turned to Mason. "You're a good man. I'm so, so sorry for doing this to you. I don't know what I would have done without you. Please look after her." I kissed Scout one last time.

"I will." He took Scout from me. "You know I'll protect her with my life." He left the bedroom.

My heart sank to my feet and shattered on the floor. I grabbed their bags, leaving the shards of my heart on the ground. I would never forget this moment when I'd lost my family, again.

Realization dawned on me that we would be separated from each other. I wouldn't be there to watch her grow up. I wouldn't be there for her first day of school, her prom night, or the look on her boyfriend's face when I showed him the tools I used for my work. That if he didn't treat Scout right, I would use the tools on him. I smiled to myself at memories I wouldn't have and wanted to drive my fist through the walls. I would keep that built-up rage to use on *him* later.

I was sure Mason would send me pictures detailing Scout's growth and her daily life. Even though I would not be there in body, I would be there in spirit and mind. And I might not be the mother she needed when she needed me, but, when she grew older, I would ensure it was safe for them to return home to me.

The back of my throat hurt as I swallowed that huge lump of regret lodged in my throat. When I could trust my voice, I reviewed the plan. "When you reach your destination, contact Glen. He'll arrange for your new ID and her birth certificate. He'll throw in a couple of credit cards and your new driver's license at no extra cost." It made me feel comfortable that Mason understood what he had to do to keep her safe. "Glen will send word to me when you're safe. For now, you cannot contact me, understand?"

Mason nodded reluctantly, but he would comply.

"Then leave as soon as you can and go somewhere far. In six months, send me a message."

Glen was someone I had met when I was young and travelling for a few months before I found Marcus. We became friends, and he showed me how to become a ghost, to live in the shadows and to never, ever get caught. Well, I only got caught because I had settled down. And it was in the town I had grown up in when I had moved here as a baby.

Mason and I approached the cab he had called earlier.

He listened in silence as I reviewed the plans for the third time, nodding diligently, rubbing Scout's back in comfort.

"I love you." I kissed him for the last time, closed the cab door and watched them drive away.

My chest tightened with a sudden pain squeezing the muscle pumping blood throughout my body. I hit the steering wheel of my car so hard I heard and felt a pop. I'd hurt my hand, a crack in the metacarpal bone near my little finger.

Screams filled my car as I let my frustrations rip from my mouth and pain from my hand and the current state of my pulverized heart.

My body would heal itself within minutes; it was my heart that worried me.

I sat in my vehicle for a very long time, my senses numb. Once I had calmed down, I pulled into traffic, heading toward my destination.

Chapter Four

My cellphone's ringtone sounded again; Ralph was urgently looking for me. I hadn't had time to call him back after I had left him alone at the institute. He was a big boy; he could get home on his own, and I would return his call when I could. I had to first meet with a madman.

The motel reminded me of a place a psycho would own, where he would take care of a guest's business for them—or just take care of them ... for good. With two floors of flea-infested rooms, I needed to go to the last room on the second level.

I found parking on the other side of the motel, climbed out and ran up the stairs nearest to my car. A man in his mid-fifties wearing baby-blue boxer briefs and a white vest was filling his ice bucket. As I passed him, he grunted profanities in a language I couldn't quite comprehend but suspected he was Russian. Tattoos covered his shoulders and chest. When his bucket was full, he stomped toward a room I had already passed.

I reached room twelve and banged on the door with the side of my fist and stood back and to the side.

This was the address they had given Mason with instructions I needed to follow. Either I came today and alone, or he would come fetch us. As the handle turned and the door opened, I un-holstered my gun and shot at the man I'd seen many times before. The silencer-equipped firearm blasted the man backward. I ducked under the window as the hail of bullets pierced the windows and door. When the shooting stopped, I peered around the doorjamb and saw another one of his goons in my line of sight and fired, hitting him in the head.

The man expelled his last breath, crashing into the wall behind him.

"Blaire! Stop shooting," he growled.

"You started this, Demetri. I told you to leave me the fuck alone." I pushed open the door but was still on my haunches as the bullet flew over my head. I fired in the direction of the spark and heard gurgling sounds.

"Blaire ..." Demetri said behind me.

As I rose, he grabbed me from behind, squeezing me against his body. We entered the room where he pushed me against the wall and sniffed my neck, causing all the hairs to stand on end. "You still smell the same as that first time." He kissed the nape of my neck.

I struggled in his arms. "Let me go." I head-butted him, causing an ache at the back of my head.

He threw me to the floor as he nursed his bleeding nose.

I landed with a hard thump on the carpet and crawled away from him.

"Still a delicious ass," he growled again with a predatory gleam in his eye and edged closer.

I aimed my gun at him, at his face.

"I wouldn't do that if I were you."

"Yeah, why not?"

A click sounded to my side, and another of his men pointed his gun at me.

"Checkmate, lil' darlin'," Demetri said as he sat on the sofa near me. "Lower your gun, Blaire. No one will hurt you. Yet." He grinned and tended to his bleeding nose.

My arms shook from keeping my gun pointed at his face, but I didn't lower it. My gaze flitted from him to the man who aimed his gun at my head. I could shoot Demetri and be happy if I died. At least Scout would be safe from his hands.

Demetri waved his hand at the man to lower his weapon. "See, no one else has to die today." He scanned the room, surveying the body count. I'd already killed two of his men and injured a third. "You've been a hard lady to track down, my pretty."

"Don't call me that. I'm nothing of yours. Never have, never will be."

He snorted. "You never gave it a chance. You ran away before I could show you my world."

I chortled in response. "Your world? The one where you killed my aunt? No. Thank. You."

"Those were rumors. I did not kill your aunt." Dare I say, he looked hurt by the accusation.

"Then what really happened to my aunt?"

"I think it was an accident."

I laughed sarcastically. "You *think* it was an accident? Is that what you're going with?"

"I loved her—"

"Loved? Then what were you trying to do with me? I was thirteen, Demetri."

He lowered his head. Was that shame? No, that couldn't be ...

"It was wrong of me to kiss you like that and to say those words. I know that now. I've been sober since your aunt—" He wiped his eyes dry.

I frowned at the poor display of endearment. "Don't give me those crocodile tears. I mean, come on! Does anyone believe this crap?" I asked, scanning the room, but only one goon stood beside me.

"Your aunt ..." He stared at me as if contemplating whether he should say anything further. "She killed herself."

"You're lying!"

"I swear."

I squeezed my eyes tight. "Why?" I shook my head. "Why would she kill herself?"

"She was going through some things, and I guess I'm partly to blame because of the other women. But she ... hurt herself."

I couldn't believe it. Didn't want to believe it. I knew my aunt didn't want to leave the house and occasionally stayed in her pajamas. But there were days when she felt okay and went out for walks. But I'd never considered she was so bad that she would hurt herself.

"Let's not dwell on the past. What do you want with me, and why now?"

"I've been searching for you for a long time, to see if you'd ever change your mind. About me. But after Laine, well, I guess things changed. Priorities changed." He shrugged. "It's your daughter I want."

I was almost hyperventilating but hiding it well underneath a frown. "No."

"She's very special." Demetri went to the kitchen counter and leafed through pages. "You don't know?"

I shook my head. "Know what?"

Satisfied with my answer, he nodded once. "Let's just say, she's very important."

"Why? She's only a baby."

"Are you telling me you really don't know the powers she possesses?"

I shook my head.

"It's indescribable."

I pursed my lips. "She possesses no power. She's human."

He leered at me, sniffing the air.

"You can sniff all you want, dog. I'm telling you the truth. Whoever gave you this information is deliriously ill-informed. I would know if she was magical. I'm her mother. Besides, I sent her away. She's gone. Not even I will find her."

Demetri bunched his hands into fists and slammed them hard on the counter as the side of his neck pulsed. "You're lying!"

I eyed the man on my left while he diverted his attention toward Demetri. I aimed my gun at his face and pulled the trigger.

His head exploded into a million pieces and splashed against the wall behind him. His body rocked. Just when I thought he would fall toward the wall; he fell on top of me.

I pushed on the dead weight, but the man was large and heavy. Blood from his neck splattered across my chest, and, with one solid heave, I pushed him off me.

As I stood, Demetri crashed into me, and we flew through the soft wall and into the next bedroom.

Demetri had partially shifted into his powerful wolf, and his yellow eyes glowed down at me while his large, sharp, toothy mouth bit down, gnawing on my right forearm.

Twisting my body to the side, I pulled my knife from my ankle sheath and stabbed him in the neck. My knife slashed through his soft flesh like butter. His blood sprayed across my face, momentarily blinding me. With my free hand, I wiped my eyes clean.

Demetri yelped and unclenched his massive jaw from my arm. He howled as he wrapped his large claws around my neck, his nails digging into my skin.

I partially shifted into my saber-animal; soft white fur flowed over my hands, my fingers grew longer, my nails sharper, and a low growl trickled from my lips. I dug my claws into his arms, trying to keep him away from me.

His eyes widened as he saw my large claws and gasped. "But ... When?"

Instead of answering, I syphoned fire from my box of tricks I kept metaphysically locked behind my shield, and I pushed it into Demetri as hard and as fast as I could.

He cried out in pain, howled, growled and eventually pushed away from me. His clothing burst into flames, and the smell of burning flesh assaulted my nose. Demetri ripped the clothing free from his body as he shifted into his wolf form—not only to remove the clothing but to heal the burns—as his large snout was snapping. He backed away from me until his tail swept against the broken wall we had just crashed through.

"Hide her well, Blaire, for when you see me again, you best be better armed." And then he ran out the door.

Sirens wailed in the distance. I fisted my claws, and they reverted to my normal hands. I needed to leave the motel room, but, with the cops on their way, I was sure they would open fire on me if I walked out the front door looking like a zombie with brain and blood on me. The only option I had was to get out the bedroom window.

I climbed out and jumped to the first-floor fire escape. Someone had parked their vehicle behind the motel and directly under me. I climbed over the railing, jumped and landed on the roof, denting it slightly before sliding to the ground.

Shouting started upstairs as I ran for the corner and scaled the wall into someone's back yard. I casually passed the washing line and grabbed the closest dry shirt. I pulled my blood-soaked top over my head and wiped off as much blood as possible. I threw the bloody shirt in the trash can and pulled on the clean t-shirt. Hiding behind a fence, I glanced down to see that the shirt ended just above my bellybutton with RoboCop holding his weapon in one hand, with a speech bubble that read, *Dead or alive, you're coming with me!* Yeah, that's how I felt right about now.

The chaos that had erupted a few minutes ago at the motel intensified now that the cops swarmed the place. They must have thought a human was in there with the monsters, because they would never have reacted like that if they knew it was just us monsters. That man with the ice bucket must have called the cops on us. The screaming from the neighbors had finally ended, but the hum of the cop car engines was still audible, and the blue and red lights flashed against the walls, like fireworks.

I couldn't fetch my vehicle with the motel swarmed. I would have to fetch it later once the shit had died down.

Chapter Five

My cellphone chimed sounded for the umpteenth time. As I dialed Ralph's number, the battery died. Cursing loudly, I walked to the nearest payphone, inserted a quarter and dialed his number.

"Where the hell are you?" he growled into the phone.

"Hi, Ralph. How are you?"

"Don't give me that crap. I can't believe you left me there, Blaire."

"It was an emergency. I had to go." I pinched the bridge of my nose with my index finger and thumb. "I'm sorry. I mean it."

"Where's my car?"

"Still at my place."

"Come, fetch me."

"You're still there?"

"Where else would I be? You left with my car."

"Um, it'll take some time."

"Why?"

"I left my purse in my vehicle, so I can't catch a cab home."

"Where's your car?"

"At a motel."

"Why is it at a motel? And why can't you get it?"

"I can't go back and fetch it just yet."

"What did you do?" he asked, his tone knowing.

"I'll tell you later."

"Where are you?"

"At a payphone."

He sighed. He knew I wasn't about to say something over a public phone that would come back to bite me in the ass.

"How long will it take you?" he asked, sounding tired.

"About two hours."

"Are you walking back to your house?"

"Yep."

He sighed. "Fine. I'll meet you at your house, then we can drive together to fetch your car."

"Fine." I hung up on him before he could continue with his reprimands. I had a long walk home ahead of me.

The walk to my place was uneventful, thank heavens. I didn't think I could have stomached any more drama for one day. The entire walk I prayed Scout and Mason were okay. I had to believe they would get out of Sterling Meadow safely. Mason was a good man; he would take great care of her. Just thinking of Scout made my chest tighten. From today on, I wouldn't be able to see her as often as I wanted anymore, our time together restricted to when and where it would be safe enough to see her.

My mind kept wondering whether I should've gone with them, just picked up my stuff and left. I was due a vacation anyway. Then Demetri's words lingered in my mind. *Hide her well, Blaire, for when you see me again, you best be better armed.* I shuddered.

Demetri was a werewolf, and whoever he had joined forces with knew about Scout, knew of her abilities. I was dumb to think I could hide her forever. It would seem that forever was now and hitting us with all its force, like a slap in my face for good measure.

We had to be better prepared.

Now that I knew they were after me, after her, they would come at me again. And again. Until they either had her or me.

Marcus and Ralph needed to prepare as well. We needed more firepower, the best weapons money could buy with the best ammunition technology could offer—silver tips, serum-filled bullets, arrows; we had to get them all.

Marcus was a were-lion, so he didn't really need anything. He could attack and rip heads off bodies and shoot, but he wasn't a fighter. He had quit sparring with us when I knocked him on his ass. He was a flake, a lazy flake, and he was our partner more than our boss. And sometimes, he could even be our friend. But not often.

We needed secret basements to store all the weapons we were about to acquire, a place where we could hide in plain sight and, if required, come out with our guns blazing.

As I turned the corner, I saw Ralph's large frame in the dusk light. I could feel the anger radiate off him. As I neared, I raised my hand to stop him before he could say anything more. "Not now, Ralph, please. I've had a fucking shitty day."

His hard expression softened. "What happened?" He noticed the kids shirt I was wearing but was kind enough not to joke about it.

"Mason had to take Scout out of here," I said, choking back tears.

"What? Why?" He reached for me but I stepped away from him.

I grabbed my spare key from the plastic rock in my garden and opened the front door then returned the key to its plastic home. "Someone tried to take Scout, and I had to neutralize the attack."

"I don't like the sound of that. I could have helped you."

"I know. Thanks." I tried to smile. I was grateful to have Ralph as my partner. "I had to do this on my own."

"Do you want to talk about it?"

I shook my head and flicked on the lights. In the kitchen, I switched on the coffee machine and grabbed two mugs. I needed to change the subject before I cried. "Did you speak to our little vampire squatter?"

"No. When you left, Dr. Hilling yelled for me. He saw you leave and was concerned something had happened to me, because you didn't answer him as you left."

The tantalizing smell of coffee made my mouth water. "I didn't realize he was talking to me. All I knew was I had to get home."

"Yeah. I guessed whatever had happened must have spooked you, because you've never stormed off like that before."

I apologized as I poured us each a mug of delicious hot coffee and handed him his mug. "We should go back and find the vamp."

"Now? Are you up to it?"

"Not really, but I need to keep busy." The numbness had returned, and I didn't like it one bit. Keeping my head in the case was the only thing that would keep me from losing it completely. If I lost control, it would only spell the end for me.

"Will Mason let you know when he arrives at his destination?"

"I won't be hearing from them for a while."

"Shit. Are they really gone? As in, *forever*?"

I nodded and sipped my coffee, allowing the steam to burn my watery eyes. I swallowed the liquid, sucked in moist air and exhaled audibly. "I'll hear from him in a few months once things around here have settled."

"I'm sorry." He squeezed my shoulder.

"Right. Let's get going. Here are your keys."

I went into my room and ignored the mess as best I could and grabbed a fresh shirt. Once I was dressed, I entered the living room. "Will you take me to fetch my car, so I can drop it back here? Or I can drive my car, then you don't have to come back here before you go home once we're done."

"No way. After a day you've had, you're driving with me. Just promise you won't commandeer my vehicle and leave me there again." He snickered, setting his empty mug on the counter and gently pushed me toward the front door.

The sun had set, and darkness surrounded the motel as it came into view. Ralph parked across the street and killed the engine. From where we sat, we could see the yellow police tape covering the front door to the room I had shot up when defending myself against Demetri's goons. Officers were still walking around.

"Shit!" I slapped the dashboard.

"You can still get your car."

"My fingerprints are all over that place."

"Ask that vamp buddy of yours, the one I'm yet to meet.

Let him bedazzle the cops, so you can retrieve the evidence. It would be like you never even existed."

That wasn't a bad idea. My cell battery was still flat, so I asked Ralph to take me to the same payphone I had called him from earlier.

I knew his number by heart, and he answered on the fourth ring. "What!"

"Hey, grumpy old man. It's me."

"Kitten, to what do I owe the pleasure?" he purred even though he still sounded gruff.

"I need your help." I gave him a short version of what had happened.

"I can't keep doing this for you. The cops will suspect something is up."

I sighed into the mouthpiece. "Last time. Please. You know they can't investigate me." I pouted even though I knew he couldn't see me, but I'm damn sure he could hear it with those super-vampire ears of his.

"I know. The last thing you need is someone digging up the past."

"Thanks. You're the best."

"I know." I could hear him smile through his words. "Come see me tomorrow night. Then you tell me everything."

"Sure."

When Ralph drove me back to the motel, fewer policemen were patrolling.

As I opened the door, Ralph asked, "What's your connection to this vampire?"

"You know I don't enjoy talking about my past." I glared at him. "And he is part of my past."

He nodded then stared at his hands.

I sighed. "Fine. He and my mom had a quick fling after

my dad passed away. Since then, he has been looking after me on and off again. Or rather, whenever he's in town."

"But you won't tell me his name?"

My answer to that was slamming the car door shut. I kept my eyes on the men and women in uniform as I maneuvered around the various vehicles and, as calmly and quietly as I could, climbed into mine. I didn't think anyone saw or heard me as I started her and merged into traffic. I glanced in the rearview mirror, but no one was jumping up and down in the road yelling for me to stop or calling for backup.

Ralph followed me to my house to leave my car there, so we could drive in one car back to the institute.

Now was the best time to have a word with the night crawlers.

Chapter Six

"Only four lights are on in that place. No wonder they keep losing children."

Ralph parked the car. "Please don't piss anyone off, Blaire."

"Yeah, yeah. I'll try." I grinned. "How about we ignore them completely and just go into the forest? Maybe we'll surprise whoever is really doing the bad things."

Ralph nodded then held his finger to his lips as we entered the front yard that led up the steps to the institute's entrance. We slipped through the side gate without being seen, exited through the back gate and entered the forest beyond.

The night was alive; leaves rustled nearby, insects hummed, lizards scampered up the bark of trees, and our feet crunched on dry leaves and twigs. I turned to glance at the monstrous institute, and the moon greeted me with a twinkling wink as its silver light cascaded onto the windows. I was meant to be on my monthly dinner date with Mason, and tonight had the perfect moonlight. I could almost taste the Italian food on my tongue. A knot formed in the base of my stomach. I could only hope they were out safely.

Right, I had to concentrate on the case. And before us was the institute with a silhouette moving behind a curtain. The figure stopped for a heartbeat, as if staring down at us, then moved on. A shudder slid through me, like ice down my back; he knew we were out here.

We moved as quietly as we could in the darkness until we reached the shed we had found earlier that afternoon. Sand covered the dead fire, and the coffin and clothing were gone.

"Maybe he moved?"

"Duh, let's look here." I pointed to a disturbed area behind the shed.

I squeezed the grip of the gun in my right hand and the handle of the knife in my left. With my left arm in the air to protect my face from the branches, I led the way. Ralph had drawn his gun, ready to protect my back while I protected the front.

Cold air whooshed passed me, and I halted. Ralph stopped so close behind me that I could feel his warm breath on my neck. The cold air whooshed passed again; the blur was fast, but I saw it and threw my knife at it.

It crashed to the ground as shrill cries pierced the silent night. "Get it out of me!" Then, as if his injuries were stopping him from masking his true self, more of him appeared as he tried pulling the knife from his back.

Ralph pushed his boot onto one shoulder blade as I leaned into his other with my right knee. We would keep him face down and in place until after we'd asked him questions. He turned his face to the side to stare up at me and hissed.

"Hold still so I can remove the knife, baby vamp." I

sensed he was a new vampire, about twenty years old and not hundreds. But he was powerful enough to mask his body from us with his speed.

"I'm not a baby vamp." He hissed again.

"Well, stop acting like one then." I yanked the knife out of his back, and he hissed louder in pain. I stood slowly and stepped away from him.

Ralph kept his boot on his back.

"Were you the one sleeping in the shed?" I asked. We had already seen him in his coffin, but I wanted to get a sense of any telltale signs when he was lying.

He nodded. It was the truth.

"Why were you hiding from us just now?"

"I didn't know who you were or what you would do to me." He didn't flinch or cast his eyes to the side; he told the truth.

"Are you taking the children from the institute?"

He averted his eyes and shook his head.

"What are you doing sleeping in the forest? It's dangerous to sleep in your coffin without magic to protect you. Anyone could've come into your shed and thrown you into the daylight. It tempted us." I smiled menacingly.

"After they destroyed my master, I had nowhere else to go."

I felt my frown deepen. "Baby vampires usually die with their masters. Why didn't you?"

He shrugged.

"I don't believe you, baby vamp. What's your name?"

"Ethan, and I don't care if you believe me or not." He grunted, tried to sit up, but Ralph's large boot kept him down. Ralph might only be a human, but he was tough as nails and strong.

"I'm Blaire, and that's Ralph. Take your foot off him, Ralph, and help him up."

A blond-haired, blue-eyed boy stood before us. He tried to rub his back from the knife wound but couldn't reach it.

"Slow healer?"

He blushed, nodding.

"Start from the beginning, Ethan. What happened to your master, and why are you sleeping in the forest?"

Ethan explained how he and his master used to stay a few miles from the institute. A man full of scales, who they assumed to be a were-lizard of sorts, had visited them. The lizard-man had requested his master's company; they had spoken in hushed tones, so he never knew the reason the lizard-man had needed his master. But the two men had left together, and that was the last he saw of his master—alive. Then two days later, he had awoken as the night kissed the air to find his master's shell of a body withered and torn, his life essence sucked right out of him. A few days later, he had returned home after hunting to find the roof sliced off. He knew it was unsafe for him to stay there, so he'd left, found the shed and had been staying there since.

"Describe the man who visited you and your master."

"He was about as tall as you." Ethan pointed at me. "He had dark hair and a ponytail, scales covered the skin that was visible and he had an odd odor."

Ethan had just described someone who looked like Dr. Hilling. Either Ethan was lying and was blaming Dr. Hilling, or Dr. Hilling was guilty of something, and we needed to figure it out.

"Describe the smell."

"I don't know, but it was a combination of vinegar, dirty water, and sulfur."

Ugh, that reminded me vaguely of sewage water.

"Thanks, Ethan. Do you know of anyone else who is living in the forest or walks through it regularly?"

He shook his head. "Maybe during the day but not while I'm awake at night. I would have smelled them if they had come anywhere near me."

"Have you seen any kids around? We found kid's clothing near your camp."

"I haven't. That clothing is what I found." He scowled. "I don't even like kids."

"Get out of the forest. It's not safe for young vampires to stay here, and especially not alone."

His blue eyes twinkled in the moonlight, but I focused on his nose. I didn't know what other powers he held, and I didn't want to take a chance either. It's always safer to look at their noses, just in case. Although the twinkling kept grabbing my attention.

"Where else can I go?"

"The city. Go mingle with your own kind. Heaven knows there are enough of you guys. Start at the clubs and make friends. I'm sure one master will take you in and blood oath you."

He nodded then left—a blur to be reckoned with.

"Let's check out the institute again," I said to Ralph.

He grunted. "He was lying, you know."

"I know." I winked at him and cleaned the knife I had removed from Ethan's back. "He'll be back. And when he does, we'll be ready for him." I sheathed the blade in place.

We took a scenic tour of the forest before we circled back to the institute. From what we could tell, no one else was in the area. The institute stood before us in all its splendor, the beast of a place that housed young orphans. My thoughts drifted to Scout again, and I already missed her. We stared at the place, just listening.

"It's awfully quiet." Ralph checked his watch. "It's only eight o'clock."

"Yeah, I don't like it either."

"What are you doing?"

I flinched at the loud voice to our left.

Even Ralph was caught off guard, but he was at least quick enough to draw his gun and aim it in the voice's direction.

A light blinded me. I lifted my hand to protect my eyes.

"Blaire? Ralph? What are you doing here at this time of the evening?" Dr. Hilling approached us, lowering his flashlight beam to the ground.

"Our job, unless you prefer that we leave, and you can solve your own mystery." With Ethan giving us some information that may or may not be true, I knew we couldn't accept Dr. Hilling at his word. We needed concrete evidence where the truth would be revealed. Now all we had to do was find it.

Dr. Hilling grunted. "No, I need you to solve it now. It's been days already. Why is it taking so long?"

I rolled my eyes and was grateful no one could see me do it. "Would you mind if we had free rein to walk around the institute?"

"Sure, but I'll walk with you." He nodded, pursing his lips.

Not exactly free rein if he was with us, but we would welcome his hospitality. Ralph walked ahead as we approached the left side of the institute where adjoining rooms with white doors and faced brick walls. Ralph pulled on the first door, but it didn't budge.

"Here, let me open it for you." Dr. Hilling unlocked the wooden door.

Ralph flicked on the light switch to reveal a storeroom

filled with buckets, cleaning materials, and a few pieces of old furniture. At the next room, Dr. Hilling used another key on his chain to unlock the door.

"These rooms used to be a horse stable in the old days. Then, a few years ago, we converted them into storerooms for things we couldn't keep in the institute."

The second room we entered was used to wash the laundry. Two industrial-sized washing machines and tumble dryers stood against the walls, with shelves above them stacked with clean linen and laundry detergents. The room smelled like fresh cotton.

The third room didn't want to open at all. The key turned, but then it got stuck.

Ralph gently pushed Dr. Hilling to one side and slammed open the door with his right shoulder.

Dr. Hilling grunted at the obvious intrusion of his personal space, but Ralph was losing patience, as was I.

Once the light flickered on, even Ralph paled. "What is this, Dr. Hilling?"

"My great-grandfather's surgery room."

I frowned. "He was a surgeon?"

"Yes. He performed minor procedures, such as dental work, and even delivered a baby here."

I gasped and shut my mouth quickly and walked farther inside the room. "Whose baby did he help deliver, if only children were living at the institute?" I turned to stare at the doctor, hiding my anger.

"An employee. In those days, it would've taken quite some time to get to any medical center. My great-grandfather checked the children's teeth and ensured they were healthy. Everything else was for the nurses, orderlies, or matrons."

A distinct smell assaulted my nose, and I shivered. It had

that disinfectant sterile hospital stench along with an old copper coin undertone to let me know blood had been spilt. The blood might have been removed, but it always seeped between the cracks.

One side of the room featured shelves filled with various surgical instruments that hadn't been cleaned in decades. Against the far wall was a shiny silver surgical table with clean clamps, forceps, scalpels, a speculum, and even a bone cutter on a tray. They seemed relatively new—or rarely used. It was a stark contrast to the ancient instruments on the other side of the room.

"Why does this room look like it's being used?"

Dr. Hilling exhaled loudly. "We've updated the equipment in case of emergencies. Nobody is using it. As you saw earlier, I struggled to open the door. I don't think anyone has been coming in here. If anyone is, it's without my knowledge."

I felt his anger swirl around me as his power flared up a notch.

"Who else has keys to these doors?" I continued staring at the surgical table with the instruments. The things someone with the right knowledge could do with those items could hurt, or help, depending on their flavor of twisted.

"Only a handful of staff have access to these rooms."

A loud scream echoed from within the institute. The lights flickered on and off, followed by more screaming. We ran toward the back door of the institute. As we entered, a large orderly dark as midnight and built like a mountain greeted us, carrying the missing girl from the evening before. A trail of blood marked his descent.

"What happened, Ormondo?" Dr. Hilling asked, flustered and clearly surprised.

Ormondo halted, tears streaking his face. "She's still alive, Dr. Hilling, but she needs your help now."

"Bring her in here."

We followed Dr. Hilling to a room off the hallway with two beds against each side wall and a medicine cabinet between them. It seemed to be a sickbay for the children.

Ormondo gently placed the girl on one bed as Dr. Hilling grabbed the first-aid kit.

The unconscious girl had a head wound and cuts down both arms, like someone had clawed at her as she tried to get away. I shuddered just thinking what she must have endured for an entire day. At least she was returned, but we had no idea what state she would be in if she woke.

"Her wounds seem to be superficial." Dr. Hilling checked the poor girl to ensure her wounds had stopped bleeding.

As I stared at the gaping wound on her head, it knitted together. A were-animal? I felt my mouth open as I realized the institute was for those children whose human parents had abandoned, because they were *different*. The girl was healing herself without the need to shift into her beast. Her eyes were on mine, and concern flashed in them as she realized I knew what she was.

"She's a shifter?" I whispered, but it still came out loud enough for everyone to hear.

Dr. Hilling nodded.

"Are they all gifted?" I asked, opting for the word gifted instead of animal; it was polite. And she was only a child who was already broken by the parents who had deserted her. She didn't need another adult to remind her of who or what she was.

Dr. Hilling stopped what he was doing and stared at me for the longest time, the third membrane closing over his eyes then returning to its hiding place underneath his eyelid. He did it slowly, so I could see it properly. He wanted us to know what he was. Perhaps he trusted us.

"Which shifter are you, Doctor?" I asked carefully. Powerful beasts surrounded us, and, as much as I could take them on, I couldn't. They only knew me as a human, no one could know what I truly was.

"Crocodile. Ormondo is a bear. Jessica is our swan. I can go on and on, if you wish. We're all alike, yet we're different."

"You protect all were-babies whose parents abandoned them?"

Dr. Hilling nodded.

A sudden pang of guilt hit me, all those thoughts I had about him. Meanwhile, all he wanted to do was protect them. But that didn't explain why he was embezzling money.

"What about the money going into your private bank account?"

"You didn't really hurt your leg earlier today, did you?"

More guilt shook my very core. He already knew. I didn't have to lie; he could smell it. I nodded.

"Blackmail. If you went through all the documents, you would've seen the money I transferred into my account was rerouted into the blackmailer's."

"I was running out of time."

He grunted. "So it would seem."

"Do you have any idea who it is?"

He shook his head. "Just that they keep wanting more and more." He bunched his hands into fists, and dark-green scales sprouted over his neck and face. The scales glistened in the light then disappeared as quickly as they had appeared.

"Do you think he's hurting the children?"

"Of course, he is."

"But why?"

"That's why I hired you, Blaire. You need to find what he has been doing with them and stop him before he hurts any more of my children."

My children—that was a very possessive way to phrase it. Unless he loved them like his own. Regardless, we needed to find out who this person was and why he was taking the kids. I suspected whoever he was worked with Ethan. We just needed to find Ethan, follow him, and then maybe we could catch the big, bad monster.

I stared at Dr. Hilling as his skin moved and glistened with dark green scales. It reminded me of a Mexican wave. I snapped out of the trance of shiny scales and faced Ormondo. "Where did you find her?"

"Under a bed."

"Which bed? Can you show us?"

"He had piercing blue eyes," the girl said as she sat eerily upright from the bed, reminding me of a zombie rising from the grave. Her dark-rimmed eyes were wide as saucers, her skin pale. She was in shock.

Everyone turned to face the little girl.

"I knew it," Ralph growled his frustrations beside me. "We should've killed the fanger when we had the chance."

"You know who it is?" Dr. Hilling asked in an accusatory tone.

"We met him earlier tonight. He was wandering around outside near a shed. He has the power of speed and to mask himself."

"You need to find him, Blaire. If it's him and he's doing this, you have to stop him."

I nodded in agreement.

A staff member stayed behind with the girl while the rest of us followed Ormondo to the spot where he had found her.

"This is the older kid's dorm, and I found her under that bed." Ormondo pointed to a bed in the far corner near an open window. The wind blew the pastel blue curtains inside the room.

Ralph and I bent to look under the bed at the same time. Blood pooled on the floor with smudge marks. I could only assume it had happened when Ormondo had picked up the girl from under the bed. I glanced at Ralph; he stared back at me. Then we stood at the same time and approached the open window.

"He doesn't know the layout of the rooms too well, otherwise he would've left her in her room," I speculated. "He flew up here with the child and left her under the bed —any bed, really. He needed a bit of a head start before someone found her, then he flew out again." I stared out the window, but nothing beastly moved about. It was only nature in all its glory.

"But why? He could've just drained her and left her body somewhere for someone to find her."

"I don't know, Dr. Hilling. Which reminds me, are there any other properties nearby?"

"Only the old mansion but nobody has lived there in years. It's only an outer shell now."

"Could either yourself or one of your staff take us there?"

Chapter Seven

My stomach twisted as I stared at the mansion. In the eerie moonlight, the outside walls looked like large claws had scraped them, as the paint flaked off it. All the windows had shattered, and the door hung on one hinge. It flapped against the doorjamb with a loud *thump, thump*. All the hairs on my body stood on end. All we needed now was Frankenstein's monster to jump from the doorway and rip out our throats. And the best part was, we were going inside. How stupid were we?

This must be the place Ethan had mentioned, but we knew he was a liar. We really couldn't know whether he honestly lived here or not with a master he may or may not have had.

Dr. Hilling was kind enough to bring us to the abandoned mansion himself. It would seem he wanted to assist us in finding the culprit, perhaps hurt the monster himself.

Ralph was already opening the front door. It creaked loud enough to alert anyone inside.

Salvation

I entered the weathered porch. The wood creaked louder underfoot as I approached the door.

"It feels like a Halloween gag," Ralph said nervously.

"Yeah, I'm in the mood to blast some heads. But, for real," I said sinisterly, un-holstering my gun. With my other hand, I activated the flashlight and pointed the beam inside the mouth of the mansion.

Ralph's light came on next and shone in the opposite direction, so we could have a good look inside. The living room was still full of things. Whoever had lived here had left in a hurry. All the furniture was still here but broken by time and the elements. Amazingly, nobody had stolen anything; they only broke the windows and left markings on the walls. When I glanced behind me, I noted it was only Ralph and me.

"Isn't Dr. Hilling joining us?"

"No. I think he fears this house." Ralph chuckled.

"I'm not scared!" Dr. Hilling yelled from outside. "I'll wait here in case someone tries to escape, so I can stop them."

"Okay, thanks!" I yelled back and swallowed a giggle. I was sure it scared him. Shifters had super hearing, and Dr. Hilling was no different.

Ralph shone his light in my face.

I rolled my eyes, which made him chuckle again.

"Try the basement!" Dr. Hilling called out again.

"Okay, we will! You can stop barking orders at us. We know what we are doing!"

If anyone was here, they would've left the moment we had entered the house. Plus, we were speaking so loudly.

"Come, Ralph, let's check the rest of the rooms before going to the kitchen."

We searched the downstairs rooms, and they all seemed

ghostly, similar to the living room. Everything was still in place, just sun faded and weatherworn. The staircase ascended into the sky; the entire roof and the upstairs rooms were missing, like a giant with a machete had sliced the house in half and took the roof with him as he walked past. I knew trolls lived in the area, but none were so large they could physically do that. But, with this being the real world, humans still weren't aware of certain things.

We reached the kitchen, and I opened the door that led into the basement. I said a silent prayer, hoping some wine racks were downstairs; I was feeling rather parched and could do with a glass of wine right about now. This mansion's owner must have entertained guests.

I stood in the doorjamb and listened.

"You scared?"

"No, I'm just listening, you brute. There's nothing wrong with being cautious."

What I didn't tell Ralph was something was calling me downstairs, and I wanted to first wait and see if I could hear or *feel* anything else. It's hard to describe, but it was *something*, and it was pulling me down there. Being my own flavor of monster, I never ignored those feelings I had. Ever. They had saved my hide once or twice, or twenty times already.

"Come, woman. Do your job. We have monsters to kill."

"Ugh, chauvinist," I replied, laughing.

Ralph nudged my side and went ahead of me. Out of habit, he flicked the wall light switch, but naturally, nothing happened. The wooden steps creaked underfoot as we descended the steps. We reached the bottom, and the smell of ammonia assaulted my nose, and my eyes watered.

The flashlights beams revealed a surgical room with expensive medical equipment, beds with stirrups, cleaning equipment, a table with clean clamps, forceps, scalpels, about fifty bottles filled with various solutions, and different sized needles.

"Ugh, another room that gives me the creeps." I inspected a scalpel. "It's awfully clean, and whoever has been down here seems very comfortable to leave this equipment with no one watching it."

"Yep," Ralph mumbled as he moved to survey the far side of the room.

I stood in one spot and moved my beam around the room. I'd had enough monsters jump out at me because I didn't search the room properly. But fortunately, no one else was down here with us.

Whoever used this place had already vacated, or they had a secret hiding spot somewhere—but I couldn't see it. "We should take this stuff with us. If we can't find or stop them, we might as well put a dent in their plans."

"Yeah, sure, but what I can't figure out is, why is a vampire experimenting on shifters? That's if it is Ethan."

"When we find him, ask."

"No need to be sarcastic."

"Sorry, not sorry."

Ralph elbowed my side as he passed me, not liking my bantering. He could dish it but didn't enjoy being served.

We scoured the basement for any other clues. Our light beams illuminated the various shelves with medical items and bottles, the equipment, and even the walls. But nothing else was down here, and no secret tunnels.

"Maybe the vampire only brings the children, and someone else performs the actual experimenting," I said.

"Hmm, maybe."

Once we had determined nothing else was down here, we ascended the steps. We had to broaden our search and not just limit it to the institute and the mansion. Something else could be deep in the forest and between the two buildings.

Once we were outside, Dr. Hilling came around the side of the mansion. "Nothing's back there."

"Ralph and I will walk back to the institute."

Dr. Hilling's eyes widened. "That's a five-mile walk."

"It's still early evening, and we need to see the terrain that surrounds both properties. Who knows, perhaps we'll see something."

"Fine. I'll give you two hours, but if you aren't back by then, I'll send a search party."

"Thanks, but we'll be fine."

We watched Dr. Hilling head to his car, his ass swaying and wobbling with each step. He climbed into his old black Lincoln and drove off.

"You just wanted to get rid of him."

I smirked. "I really want to see the extent of the two properties. Come, let's see what we can find."

The air was pleasant as we traversed the forest that connected the mansion to the institute. Brown leaves covered the ground, which made our view between the trees easier because leafy vegetation wasn't obstructing it. The only sounds were owls and our collective breathing.

"I haven't seen any animals."

I stopped and beheld the panoramic view. "You're right. Neither have I, come to think of it." I was disappointment in myself; I should've noticed that immediately, but my mind was still on Scout and Mason leaving. If we were to catch this creep, I needed to get my mind back into the game. They were safe; I had to trust in Mason that he would do that for me.

We walked for a short time and hadn't come across anything of interest and no animals. We needed to cover more ground and quicker. "Ralph, I think we should split up. You carry on with this path while I take a wider path."

He halted and narrowed his eyes at me. "What are you up to?"

"Nothing, I swear. But it makes sense, doesn't it? We're both capable of handling ourselves in case the big, bad wolf follows us back to Granny's house."

He chuckled. "Fine."

"I'll see you later."

I moved farther to the right to take a wider path to the institute. When I thought enough distance was between us, I undressed and folded my clothing in a neat pile and hid them under branches. The shift into my saber was quick and relatively painless. I'd had years of practice and could do it without being a hostage to the full moon. Granny had said I was powerful enough to do it undetected and with ease. And the more I did it, the easier it became.

I'd discovered her, my saber, soon after Ma's murder. Little by little, every day, my anger had consumed me. Rage had filled my veins, and all I thought about was the man I wanted dead, wiped off the face of the Earth—the one who had hurt Ma and had taken her from me forever.

My saber had reared her beautiful furry white head one day when I cracked—or so it felt. I had fought with Granny about not doing my homework; it was a task I could've completed at school. The fight had been so small and irrelevant, but it had provided the cherry on top of my proverbial anger sundae. Granny had reprimanded me, and I had retorted with mean and hurtful words, like how she wasn't my mom and had no right to tell me what to do. I had grabbed my school bag and had left the house angry. My blood had been pumping through my veins at such a rate my vision had blurred, and heat had surrounded me.

Thank heavens no one else had been around. I had been on my way to school and had taken a shortcut through the park when it had happened.

All I had seen was a white explosion.

The bright light.

The burning sensation.

My first shift.

But the worst part had been all the pain, the most excruciating feeling in my then short life—bones broke, muscles stretched and pulled until they felt like I would die a slow and very painful death. Or I was begging for the Angel of Death to swoop down from wherever he was, fetch me and end all my pain.

When it had all ended, there was no more pain. I was walking on all fours with weird sounds spewing from my mouth. And I moved fast. The freedom I had felt from running was therapeutic. Freeing. The change had helped me channel my anger somewhere else. It had helped me cope with my loss. I had pushed harder as I ran, then, when I had tired and the anger had left my body, I collapsed into a heap, crying from raw emotions.

I didn't know it then, but years later, while I was studying everything I could about shifters, I realized I was one of a kind—better, stronger, more agile, and fiercer. Unfortunately, it wasn't something I could exactly brag about openly, because they considered me human—plain vanilla.

I always knew of my other witchy powers. Ma and Granny had helped me master my shield, so my flavor stayed vanilla to the rest of the mystical world. Nobody could see my *shine*. I had to hide my white light, like some dirty secret. Ma and Granny had warned me against the dangers out there. And, to protect myself, they had prepared me for my future and had taught me how to defend myself, a way I could survive.

Back in the forest and in search of the baby vampire, I was running so fast the world blurred past me. I took a wider circle back to the institute. I hadn't caught a whiff of any other creatures lurking in the night. Nor did I see any other houses or makeshift sheds where a monster could hide. Nothing seemed out of the ordinary. I turned around and ran back to my pile of clothing and dressed. I had to be quick, so I could still meet with Ralph at about the same time as he would reach the institute.

"My oh my. I'm glad I was in time for the strip show," someone said behind me.

I spun around as I clasped my bra in place. It was Ethan. I hadn't smelled his corpse approach. Vampires had a distinct earthy, bloody smell to them, and I could always sense them near me. But somehow, I couldn't smell him.

"*Hmm*, you're so beautiful, darlin'. I'm glad I came back for you," he drawled; his smile stretched lazily across his face.

I pulled on my underwear, jeans, and shirt. I sat on the ground and slipped on my socks and boots.

"Why are you getting dressed? I thought you and I could have some fun first. I won't tell, if you won't." He winked seductively.

"No thanks, baby vamp. Not interested in bloodsuckers." I pouted mockingly then stood. "You're just not my type."

"I'm *not* a baby vamp. I have lived for decades."

"What? Not centuries?" I pushed out my left hip and placed my hands on my hips.

He flew into me, and we crashed into the branches I'd used to hide my clothing. Once on the ground, he straddled my waist and pinned my forearms to the ground above my head.

"Who is your master?" I demanded.

"You don't want to know, sweetheart. He won't be as gentle as me, I can promise you that."

"What does he do with the kids?"

"*Hmm*, not sure I can trust you yet, darlin'."

"Tell me, Ethan, please," I whispered, pleading with my eyes.

When I said his name instead of *baby vamp*, he relaxed his grip on my forearms, and his shoulders sagged slightly.

"He performs tests on them. He wants to see what he can get from their powers." His shoulders relaxed, as if the confession was a weight lifted.

I was sure he had never spoken to anyone about what he was part of, and just mentioning that bit of information to me was therapeutic for him. I didn't think he enjoyed scouting for the children or bringing them to his *master*. I assumed it was something he had to do or face his death.

"How?" I ensured I kept eye contact with him to keep him comfortable. It was a little trick I had learned from a psychologist.

Ethan squeezed my wrists, contemplating his next words. "With special machines he built."

"Why is he doing this?"

"Enough!" he yelled, shaking an imaginary voice out of his head.

"Please, Ethan," I whispered. "We have to stop him. *Help me.*"

"No one can stop him." Ethan lowered his face; his lips were soft against mine. He moaned in that kiss, and it sent vibrations throughout my body. "Are you ready for some lovin'?"

"First, tell me about your master. Who is he? Where is he? Then you can have all of me and for as long as you want."

"No! I'm tired of talking about him." He kissed me again then pulled away, purring. "Your lips are so soft and so sweet."

"Help me, Ethan," I repeated, my eyes willing his cooperation.

"I *am* helping you, darlin'. If I take you to him, he'll run tests on you until he breaks you. A saber hasn't been around for centuries. You might be just what he's been looking for, the missing piece to his crazy puzzle. Do you really want to throw yourself at the devil?"

"I can defend myself."

He laughed bitterly. "Not against him, you can't. He's like no other. He's a destroyer of life to create the demons he needs." Ethan closed his eyes, shaking his head, like he was having a bad dream or memory.

I moaned under his tightening grip. "Ethan, look at me."

Ethan turned that cold stare at me, and I felt the chill run through my body. I shuddered. "Where is he? Tell me," I whispered.

"The mountains, that's all I'll say. Now time for my prize," he demanded, his words full of rage.

I would not allow him to do what he wanted with me. I slid quickly from under his hands, so I could grip his forearms instead. I needed to touch him for it to work.

His mouth dropped open in surprise then grinned, realizing I was quicker than him. I lowered my shield and opened my little box of tricks, found what I was looking for and pulled Ethan toward me.

He stared at me with lust-filled eyes.

My mouth found his, and I kissed him, my tongue parting his lips. This would be his last kiss, and I would make it one to remember. Our lips locked, and I breathed him in. I sucked in air for a long time, filling my lungs with his breath. As my lungs expanded, it felt like I would die myself.

His life drained from his body as it moved into mine.

The pulse I felt on his wrists slowed until it eventually stopped. When his lips were no longer soft against mine, I opened my eyes to see I was clutching a mummified Ethan —an empty husk. I released his arms and pushed his now light body off me.

His life essence moved within me, and I felt indestructible—godlike, for lack of a better word. I would conquer this master who was hurting children and bring him to his knees.

That power I had just used was a gift to me from a powerful voodoo priestess when I had solved her sister's murder. It came in handy, and I was grateful for having it. Closing my box of tricks and shutting my shield tight again, I stood and dusted myself off. I needed to hurry, so I could meet with Ralph at the institute.

I used Ethan's life essence swirling inside me to run the fastest I'd ever run—as a human. I blurred past trees and rocks until I arrived at the outskirts of the institute. Ralph hadn't even arrived yet. I flashed a toothy grin as I waited for him, and I wasn't even out of breath.

Twigs crunched underfoot. I turned in that direction and saw Ralph emerging from a bush he had walked through. He seemed deep in thought. I cleared my throat.

"Shit, Blaire. How did you get here so quickly?"

"I ran."

"I think you should lay off the gym for a while. You'll put me to shame one of these days."

"Did you find anything out there?"

"Nah, nothing. Whatever or whoever was out there is long gone."

"Yeah, I think so too. But we should come back in a few days, expand the search. Maybe we could check out the mountain."

He narrowed his eyes at me.

"What?"

"You saw something, didn't you?" He stared at me with clear intent, from my dusty shoes to my unkempt hair. "Why are you so dirty?"

"I tripped and fell."

He shook his head.

"What?"

"Really, after all this time, you think I'm that dumb?"

"I don't think you're dumb."

"Don't insult my intelligence." He leered at me, anger burning bright in his eyes.

"Fine. I bumped into that baby vamp."

"Here we go. I knew it! What did you do to him?"

"He is dust, okay?"

"He was our only lead!"

"He told me his master tested on the kids. I don't know exactly what that means, just that he tested on them to use as he pleases."

Ralph shuddered. "And he mentioned the mountain?"

"Yeah."

"Well, the sun will rise soon. His master will disappear underground or go to his resting place for the day. Perhaps you're right. We should return in a day or two, search the mountain areas." He glanced at the institute. "I just wish you'd share these types of things with me without me having to pry it out of you."

"Sorry." I shrugged.

"You know I don't judge you."

"Yeah, I know." I glanced away from his intense glare.

"Come, let's get out of here."

Dr. Hilling stood on the back porch, watching us approach and sipping on a cup of tea. "Find anything?"

"No, but we'll come back in a day or two. I want to research a few things before returning, if that's alright."

"Sure. We'll wait until then."

"Keep the kids safe while we're away," I said as we walked past.

Dr. Hilling grumbled something, but I didn't have the energy to press him.

Once Ralph pulled his vehicle onto the road, he asked, "Okay, so why aren't we coming back tonight?"

"I want to go to the records department first, and then I want to see Old Man."

"Okay." He nodded. "I'll chat with a buddy of mine who knows a thing or two about these mountains."

Chapter Eight

First, I went to the records department where all the blueprints were kept for our aging town, but nothing showed anything existed out there apart from the institute and the mansion. Checking the library revealed the same conclusion. We had to go out there blind, which I didn't like one bit. If what Ethan had told me was true, then his master was powerful and might destroy us before we could even think about retaliating. And, if he got a good whiff of me and knew what I was, then I would not come back from that alive.

Next, I drove around, looking for Demetri. He was a werewolf, so I stopped at the wolf pack, hoping he was there. He was an outsider and had to have the wolf king's permission to be in town and to stay. And he had to attend all pack meetings.

I doubted he would arrive, but I was here with the hopes I would see him. Plus, I knew when each of the were-animals would usually meet at their respective venues, because I kept tabs on each of them. Even though I hadn't met most of them or their leaders, I knew of them. Some had even sent us contracts on their members, but Marcus usually handled that. Ralph and I would get a yellow folder with the relevant information inside and what we needed to do and if it required further investigation, like our current case, then that's what we did.

I sat in my car and watched all the wolves approach the entrance for their weekly meeting. I didn't recognize anyone. I only knew Xavier, the wolf king.

After an hour, I turned the key to fire up the ignition, and something caught my eye. I glanced to my right, toward the edge of the forest, and saw people walking. It was strange; werewolves rarely met like that if they were supposed to be in the building for their meeting.

I turned off the ignition and climbed out my car. I followed the three men deeper into the forest, the part where only the werewolves were allowed to be. I knew I shouldn't be here, but I had to see if one of them was Demetri. Being in wolf territory was not only dangerous for me but stupid. But I had everything to gain by being here. And besides, I had already lost Scout and Mason. I shook the memories away and shoved down the emotions. Now was not the right time to be sad.

As I neared the men, one of them looked awfully similar to Demetri, except he'd shaved his dark hair close to his head. It changed the look of his face completely. It made him look harder, meaner, permanently pissed off with those dark eyes and chiseled chin. A memory of him looming over my aunt made me shudder, and my pulse thumped in my ears.

They stopped talking and sniffed the air.

Shit. I needed to calm down or risk being found. I stood

still, wiped beads of sweat from my forehead and tried to steady my breathing, which was difficult.

Through the thick tree branches I was hiding behind, I glimpsed them approaching me. I turned to see if I had any kind of escape route, but it was only this large tree I was hiding behind. Their footsteps grew louder as they got closer.

Crouching down, I lowered my shield, held my breath and dug into my chest of tricks. Shaking my head, I closed the chest again and stood. What was I doing? This is what I wanted after all; I didn't want to hurt any of them with my box of tricks. Yet. I wanted them to find me, to learn who Demetri was working for. I stepped away from the tree; I glared at the man with the shaved head. It was him.

"Blaire, so good of you to join us," Demetri purred. "I had no idea you were a shifter, darlin'. But what exactly are you? You smelled like no other when you partially shifted the other day." He was close enough to touch me, but he didn't. His friends circled me like sharks. "Even now, I can't smell what you really are." He sniffed the air round me.

"You're right," the man on my right said. "I smell it too, but I can't figure out what she is. Perhaps Cleo can help us."

"Yeah, Cleo will know what to do with her," the man on my left added.

"Who is Cleo?" I asked, my head held high. I would not allow this man to haunt my dreams any longer. To finally stand up to him was better than any therapy session.

"I see what you're trying to do, but Cleo isn't the one you seek," he chimed, happy with himself for figuring out why I had sought him out.

"Who wants my daughter? That's the least you could do," I asked, my hands bunching into fists, and I firmly planted my feet on the grass. I was ready to fight them if they attacked first.

He chuckled. "She's definitely like no other, that's for sure. Look at her, she's ready to fight us."

The other men chuckled with him.

"Hey, Demetri," someone called out, running toward us.

"Shit." Demetri sighed then whispered under his breath, "Say nothing, boys." To the approaching man, he said, "Dillon, to what do we owe the pleasure?"

"What are you three doing out here? The meeting is about to start, and you need to be there if you wish to remain in our town."

"That was my fault. Sorry. I asked them for an address for a mutual friend."

"Who the hell are you?" Dillon asked, giving me the same deadly stare he gave Demetri. "You don't smell like wolf."

"I'm nobody."

Demetri faced me again. "Blaire, go home. I'll find you." He gave me a knowing look then approached Dillon so the four of them could return to the clubhouse.

A sinking feeling stuck in my diaphragm, and I struggled to breathe. With hands on my hips and trying to steady my breathing, I headed to my car.

That was close. Too close.

Chapter Nine

The lights dimmed and soft flute music played in the background. Old Man came onto the stage to join his partner, a petite brunette wearing nothing but a thong. Old Man bowed to the audience, whispered something into his partner's ear, and she visibly relaxed. Her chest rose and fell steadily with Old Man's, her breathing completely in sync with his.

As I watched them, I noted my breathing matched theirs, and it seemed to relax me.

Old Man grabbed the jute rope and bound his partner. His delicate fingers caressed her skin on certain parts of her body that caused her to elicit pleasure across her face. He wrapped jute around her breasts, caressing a nipple as he circled her and made a beautifully intricate knot against her skin. He pulled the rope around her waist, so the rope now bound her breasts. Then he bound her right hand to her right shoulder, so her hand cupped her right cheek. He gently took her left arm and brought it behind her back and roped her in place with similar intricate knots.

His partner's eyes fluttered open, panic etched on her face. She must have had a panic attack from the tight binding.

He stood in front of her, cupping her face gently, and whispered into an ear.

Her shoulders visibly relaxed once more, and her breathing steadied as they breathed in sync with each other again.

People shifted in their seats watching the sensual show, nobody tearing away their gaze for even a second.

Old Man gathered more jute rope and helped his partner to sit on the stage. He bound her legs and feet with his unique technique, creating the beautiful knots. Once she was bound, he threaded the jute through a metal ring and hoisted her up.

Her expression reflected utter peace as she swung gently in the air.

When performing this show, the goal for Old Man was for his partner to achieve a deep therapeutic meditative state.

Heat climbed my neck and face as I watched the art of Kinbaku and felt the air swarming around me, full of sexual arousal. If Old Man wasn't like a father to me, I'd be on that stage so fast I'd give myself whiplash.

When Old Man lifted his hands, the main lights dimmed further, and the ropes glowed different colors and created a beautiful pattern against his partner as she swung gently in the air. Her expression was that of a sleeping angel, loved by all.

Everyone clapped, with some women cheering.

Old Man bowed again, signaling the end of his passionate demonstration.

"Oh god, I wish that was me. I think I'd even let him

have his way with me afterwards," the woman beside me said to her friend, and they both blushed and giggled.

"He can have us both," her friend said, "at the same time." And they laughed again.

Their lustful whispering made me smile, but they didn't notice I was sitting beside them; they only had eyes for him.

The lights came on bright enough for everyone to see where they were going as they headed toward the exit.

Old Man lowered his partner to the floor.

Her face expressed she was positively floating on cloud nine as he untied her.

A boy stood beside the girl with a pair of emergency scissors, but Old Man shook his head, waving him from her. It wasn't necessary to cut her free.

Once she was free, Old Man carried her to a private room in the back. After a few minutes, he returned, grinning at me from the stage. When the last person left, he spoke. "You finally made it to my show."

"It was beautiful," I said as I descended the stairs to meet him near the stage.

"You should try it sometime."

"Uhm, I don't know about that. I can't picture myself naked with you. You're like a dad to me. Gross."

He chuckled. "You can wear clothing, kitten. Thin, light clothing would do. I don't have to touch you anywhere you don't want to be." He raised an eyebrow. "But it would be an experience of a lifetime, and it would be my pleasure."

"I'll bet!" My grin matched his. "I think half these women will go home to ravage their partners."

"Good. Nothing's wrong with a little sensual play between consenting adults in the bedroom."

"Don't know why I didn't come see you sooner."

"It's that boy Mason. He never liked it when you came to see me."

My chest closed up. The few minutes of not thinking about Scout and the loss came rushing back.

Old Man must've noticed my discomfort at his mentioning his name. "Come, let's talk in my office."

I followed him into his office and closed the door behind me. He had a soft brown leather couch to one side, a wrought-iron desk on the opposite wall, and a bookshelf lined with old leather books.

"Come sit next to me," he purred as he sat on the couch.

I grabbed a picture frame from his desk. "I've never seen this before. Who are they?"

I noticed a small shift in his demeanor, then he resumed his stone-like stance. "They are my sons."

I burst out laughing. "What? Did you adopt grown-ass adult men? That's creepy, even for you."

"No, they're my real children."

"What?" My eyes widened. "This looks like a recent photo." I could tell by their clothing.

"It was taken a few months ago."

"Shut up." I stared at the picture again. "Are you for real, Old Man?"

"Yes, kitten. Now put that down and come sit here." His voice was commanding, and I knew I had to obey, but I had so many questions still.

"Did you turn them into vampires, and then they became your sons?" I frowned at the frame.

"No, they are my flesh and blood. One is actually the master vampire of our city."

"Léon is your son?" I felt my mouth part in a surprise *O*. Everybody knew of the handsome vampire who mastered the vampires and were-animals of Sterling Meadow. And to think he had a real *father*, whom I knew.

He nodded.

"Did Ma know you had children?"

"She knew."

"Why didn't I?" I placed the picture frame on the desk and sat beside him.

"You were young. Life was complicated enough for you. I couldn't introduce my dynamics into your young life."

"How old are they?"

"Almost eight hundred years old."

My mouth dropped open. "And the other hottie? What's his name, and where is he?"

"He works with Léon."

"Oh." I stared at him, waiting for him to elaborate, but he didn't; he just stared at me. "But you don't want to give me his name?"

He shook his head.

I frowned. "Dynamics?"

"Yes, there are dynamics at play that would be disastrous for you."

"What aren't you telling me?"

"Nothing you don't already know, Blaire. But now isn't the time to go into the details about my sons. Tell me what happened to your baby girl."

He used my real name; he only did that when he was irritated with me. I narrowed my eyes at him. "Fine. I don't believe you, but let's move on anyway."

Old Man knew most of my life history; I told him what had happened with Demetri and how Mason had to take Scout and go hide forever.

"That's good." He nodded, pleased with my decision. "If they change their names every six months, or even every year, they won't be as easy to find. And, kitten, you knew your aunt was weak. Now that you know she didn't die at Demetri's hands but her own, do you feel you have closure knowing what really happened to her or don't you believe him?"

"No! I don't believe him. I know she was weak, but still." I shrugged, admitting defeat. "I guess no one really knew what happened behind her closed doors. Anyway, I want to move on from that and find out who he's working with or for. And why they want Scout."

"Your baby girl will be powerful one day. She'll need your and Mason's protection for as long as possible. Unfortunately, I agree with you. Find out who this person is, who is hunting your child."

I nodded, swallowing the large lump until the back of my throat hurt, and I blinked back tears.

"I offer some comfort. It was easy removing all traces you were even at that wolf-infested motel."

I was grateful he'd changed the subject. I leaned over, wrapped my arms around his neck and kissed his cheek. "Thank you, Old Man. You're a powerful and ancient vampire. You only have to snap your fingers, and it's done."

"Yes, it was something like that." He chuckled.

"I'm glad I have you on my side."

He wiped the lonely tear from my cheek, and then I sat back. "How do I find out who Demetri is working for?"

"You will figure it out. You always do."

"You have such confidence in me."

He smirked, and I could've sworn I saw a twinkle in his eye, like he was proud of me. As if reading my mind, he said, "Your mom would be proud of you. No matter what you do, she is proud of you."

I smiled at the fond memories of Ma and how she had

always trusted in my gut instincts. Even though I had been so young, she had always believed in me.

I studied him—his blue eyes, salt and pepper hair, high cheekbones, and thin lips. He had looked this way ever since meeting him all those years ago. Ma had introduced him to me as *Old Man*, and I'd been calling him that ever since.

"Why have you never shared your real name with me?"

His demeanor shifted again. He seemed utterly uncomfortable then resumed his stone stance. "It's safer for you. Like you say, I am ancient, and others out there are my enemy. If they knew you had any idea who I really was, they would set their sights on you. I don't want that. Until my enemies are all dead, you shall only know me as *Old Man*. Understand?"

I bowed my head, not enjoying his reprimand.

"It's my way of keeping my promise to your mother, to protect you for as long as I can." His voice was softer, gentler, putting me at ease.

"Why didn't you take me in when Ma died, when I needed you the most?"

He stared at me with hurt reflecting in those blue eyes. "Because of the same reasons I just shared. They would've slaughtered you. And I was overseas. I had no way to fetch you." He shook his head and waved his hand. "Enough of these sad memories."

I nodded, trying not to recall those hurtful memories.

He stood. "Drink?"

"Yes, please. Your finest wine, Old Man."

"Only the best for my kitten." He went to the other side of his wrought-iron desk, pulled a light switch from the wall, and the cogs and wheels turned. The wall panel shifted, revealing a once-hidden staircase. He glanced at me over his shoulder. "Come on, all the wine is down here."

The Ulysses team needed secret hideaways similar to Old Man's. Perhaps we needed basements. I would ponder it and discuss it with Ralph.

I sprang from the couch and followed him down the dim staircase, the door closing behind us automatically. The smell of damp stone assaulted my nose as we moved deeper into the mouth of his home. I'd only been down here twice since he moved back to town, and both times it had been fun. He's a happy drunk for a vampire and always made me laugh with tears of joy streaking my face.

Once we reached the bottom, we passed a few doors. I had to peek inside as we walked. "What's this?" I asked near one doorjamb.

"That's my pleasure room."

"You kinky Old Man, you." I smiled and wiggled my eyebrows. "I knew Kinbaku was sensual play and part of your show, but I didn't know you were a full on dominant. How did I miss this room both times I was down here?"

"You were tipsy." He chuckled.

"Oh." I grinned.

Inside his playroom was a trunk near the far wall, which I could only assume was full of toys. In the middle of the room sat a table with straps on each leg, so whoever was lying down was tied down. Parallel to the table was a smaller bench with the middle raised and padded and more straps. Against the wall was a Saint Andrews cross. Hanging on hooks against the walls were floggers, spreader bars, handcuffs, shackles, and a bullwhip.

"I had no idea."

"Don't get any ideas. You're like a daughter to me."

I choked on my laugh and stared at him with a straight face, shaking my head. "No, ew, that's just gross. Never."

We left his pleasure room, traversed the hallway and

descended more steps to his cellar. Rows and rows of shelves displayed bottles of wine, champagne, and expensive whiskey.

He grabbed two crystal goblets and set them on the table in the middle of the room. "Sit," he commanded and circled the room, looking for the perfect bottle. He grabbed a dusty bottle from the top shelf. Once he wiped away all the dirt, it was lined with gold.

"We can't. It looks priceless."

"It is, but you're worth every penny." He opened the bottle and poured some in my glass first. "Taste."

I did as he ordered. The wine was heaven on my tongue —a mixture of berries, oak, vanilla, and even a hint of dark chocolate. "Hmm," I hummed as I took another sip.

His smile reached his eyes as he filled my glass then his. "Cheers, kitten."

"How did you find this place?"

"It's always been mine. I built it with my hands long before this place even became the town it is now."

"I forget you are *that* old," I teased. "I've always wondered, how were you turned? I don't think you've ever told me the story."

He stared at me over the rim of his goblet, sipping the delicious wine, and set the goblet on the table. "I guess you're ready to hear this now." He cleared his throat. "Many years ago, when Romania was different. My father was a very wealthy farmer and travelled some but not often. When I was twenty, he set forth to do some trading. Little did I know that would be the last time I'd see him alive. He became gravely ill, and, as he was dying, the men who travelled with him decided to turn back. But he was already dead by the time they returned. My father was the world to my mother, and she fell into a deep depression, while I drank way too much. Soon thereafter, my mom became ill, and she too passed. There I was, twenty-two, alone, and my father's estate was busy drying up. And all I did was drink and enjoy as many women who wanted me. Until one evening, I was lying in the gutter half naked with half a bottle of wine in my hand. I realized then life had to have more to it than what I was busy going through. I managed to get home, cleaned myself and sobered up.

"I became friends with a businessman who was visiting our town, and he helped me build my father's empire back to what it originally had been and make it my own. My fortune surpassed my father's. It would make any father proud of his son. But, as they say, the high cannot last. The businessman had lost some of his money due to debts and tried to steal mine. When I caught him, he looked me in the eyes and stabbed me in the side. There I was, lying in the gutter, again, clutching my wound as I was bleeding to death. Then a woman took pity on me. She was a goddess in the moonlight. Her hair shone like gold and her eyes the truest blue. She gave me a choice. Did I want to live or die? I chose life obviously. But, in hindsight, I didn't really understand what she was offering me or what the price was for the life she had offered.

"A couple of days later, I woke and my wounds had healed. But I was so thirsty that no amount of water or wine would quench me. Unfortunately, everything that had happened, it had given me the silver streaks you see in my hair today. It made me look much older than my twenty-eight years."

"I love your hair that color."

"Thanks, kitten. Anyway, the goddess who had kissed me explained what I was and what my new life was to become. And, as predicted, I was enraged and wanted revenge on the businessman who had sent me to the depths of my Hell. After a couple of days of not succumbing to the temptation, my bloodthirst was driving me deranged, and I had to drink, or I would die, and it would all have been for nothing. So naturally, for my first victim, I found the businessman and sucked him dry. I relished as I stared into his face as his light faded from his eyes. Those god-awful brown eyes." Old Man fisted the table, causing me to flinch and our goblets to wobble. "Sorry."

I grabbed my goblet and downed the rest of the wine. "Wow! What a story! I just can't imagine how everything must have been back in *those* days." I smiled mischievously at the emphasis.

"Much different from what they are today, that I can assure you. Back then, we lurked in the shadows, drank blood from our victims then used our vampiric wiles to help them forget what we did to them. Today, humans offer their necks to us for a slice of vampiric heaven." He wiggled his eyebrows.

"Gross." I giggled, lifting my glass for more.

"Young ladies do not ask for more. They wait patiently to be offered."

I rolled my eyes.

"I don't want to sleep alone." I felt the creases between my brows deepen. "Please, won't you stay with me?"

Old Man gently settled me into my bed, lifted the covers and tucked me in. "No. If I stayed, I'd become crispy at dawn. Then I'd be useful to no one."

I chuckled then repeated, "Crispy." I tucked my hands under my pillow as my eyelids felt heavy and closed. Just as I nodded off, it felt like I was falling, and I reached for him before I hit the ground, yelling for him to stay. "Wait!"

He took my hand, gently kissing it. "Sleep. If you want, we can do this again another night. But I need to leave."

I felt his soft lips on my cheek, and then I slept.

I woke a few hours later with a pounding headache. Swallowing hard, my mouth felt like cotton balls. I steadied myself as I climbed from the bed to use the bathroom and showered. When I was dressed and had brushed my teeth, I drank a strong cup of coffee to wake up.

I had to meet Ralph on the mountain. We were going to see if other structures existed in or near those mountains where someone could keep people hidden.

Chapter Ten

On one of the first bends up the hill, I noticed enough space to park my car alongside the road. The bend was high enough where I had the mansion in my sight and in the distance, the institute's roof visible. I heard that ghastly engine before I saw Ralph's car. He parked an inch from my bumper.

"Couldn't you have parked any closer?"

"My ass sticks out if I don't get all up and close to your goodies." He grinned.

"Funny." I rolled my eyes. "Could you get any information from your buddy?"

"Nah, he says nothing else is up here besides those two buildings. But ..." He approached the edge of the barrier. "There are caves down here." He pointed down. "We should look. If that baby vamp is correct, and his master is hiding here somewhere, then that's our way in."

"You must be joking. How will we get down there? It's a straight drop." I glanced over the railing at the fifty-foot drop. My stomach fell to my feet, and the earth below me swam in swirly waves. I stepped back, staring skyward until the world righted again.

Ralph shook his head. "After all this time, you still don't trust me."

I glared at him.

He glared back.

I burst out laughing, then he did as well.

"Come, wench. Let's take the path over there."

I squinted to where he pointed his finger. I grabbed the backpack I kept in my car for such instances and threw it over my shoulders.

"Did you bring enough water and food? We might be here the whole night."

"Yeah. I always have enough reserves just in case. Did you?"

"*Pfft*, of course." He slung his backpack over his shoulders and fastened it in front.

I followed Ralph down toward the path that would supposedly lead us to the mountain. I had to walk behind him, because it was wide enough for only one hiker at a time.

"After all these years I've lived here, I had no idea a trail was even down here."

"I doubt many people know about it. Look how overgrown the path is."

"Do you have a map or compass or something, so we know where the hell we're going?" I walked right into his backpack, my nose connecting with a zipper. "Ouch, Ralph. Did you have to stop so suddenly?" I slapped his backpack, hurting my hand.

"Blaire, how many times have we gone hiking together? I always come prepared." He sounded like my comment had hurt his feelings.

"Okay, fine. Sorry. Just move. I feel like a sitting duck out here in the open." I pushed hard against his backpack, knocking him forward, and he almost tumbled. I burst out laughing.

Ralph shook his head. "You are like a fucking schoolgirl sometimes."

"Except I know how to use these." I lifted my knives and twirled them around my fingers.

Ralph turned and proceeded to do a mock ninja move.

We both burst out laughing.

"Come, wench. Let's go." He turned and traversed the path again.

"Stop calling me that, whipping boy."

Ralph slid his sunglasses to the tip of his nose and tried to give me his best scary eyes.

"Your eyes are too pretty to be mean to me."

He walked away, chuckling.

After an hour of hiking the path, we reached a fork. Ralph retrieved his map, pointed to our location and indicated we were to follow the left-forked path, which appeared feint and hardly recognizable as a path at all, not forgetting the risk that we could stray from the original path and end up somewhere completely different. It had overgrown grass and bushes, like it hadn't been used in a very long time.

"Are you sure this way is correct?"

"Yep."

"How sure?"

"Woman, I swear, ask me one more time—"

"How sure?" I burst out laughing the moment Ralph turned to backhand me in the face. But I was too quick for him. I ducked under his arm and punched—lightly—into his side.

He doubled over in mock pain, clutching the side I had hit.

"You're getting slow in your old age, Ralph." I tapped his belly. "Huh, not as rock hard as it used to be, eh?"

"Watch yourself, little girl. One day I'll get you when you least expect it."

"Promise?" I pouted, while he guffawed at my puffed lips.

"Yeah, promise. Now come, we should be there soon."

We walked for another hour when the sky was painted with gold and yellow rays of sunshine. The mouth of a cave revealed itself as dusk followed.

The cave's darkness sent cold shivers down my spine, and I rubbed my arms. "Do you feel that?"

"What? I don't feel anything."

"Never mind."

Ralph was plain human, which meant he couldn't feel anything out of the ordinary or otherworldly. I, on the other hand, could. As we entered the cave, I felt something—sharp. It's an odd word choice, but that's how I would describe it, like knives dragging across my tender flesh and splitting it open one inch at a time. Something horrible had happened inside, and we were about to discover it. It wasn't something I could share with Ralph either. He was oblivious to my many talents, and it was my choice not to share any of it with him. It was safer for him if he thought I was normal, like him.

I switched on my flashlight as I entered.

Ralph camped often, so he always had all the right gear. When he activated his flashlight, the beam was so large and bright it illuminated the entire cave walls, and I clearly didn't need my puny one. I switched mine off and tucked it back inside my backpack.

A deep moan sounded from inside the cave.

I froze.

"Don't worry, it's just the wind. There must be an opening from somewhere up ahead."

"When did you go caving last?"

"About a month ago, when you and the family celebrated Scout's birthday."

"Oh, yes. Who did you take?"

"Amanda was last month."

"And this month?"

"Karin."

"Ugh, you are such a man-whore."

"You had your chance, baby. Besides, I give these women the best month of their lives."

"You're so gross."

"But you still love me, don't you?" Ralph bumped his hip into mine, and I nearly tripped and fell.

"Only when we work." I bumped him back.

I loved him but more like the big brother I never had. We had been attracted to each other once in the beginning of our working relationship, but I didn't want it to go any further. I enjoyed our one time together but valued our relationship as work partners more. To become lovers would've ruined what we had. He was my best friend after all. But, ever since Mason and I started dating and then I had Scout, he had been offering himself to all women—every month, it was a different one. I worried about him. I didn't want to see him get hurt.

At first, the cave before us was large. Then, the farther we went, the narrower, darker, and smaller it became. The farther we explored, the damper the walls and the sweeter the air.

We followed Ralph's bright light until we reached a dead end.

I sighed, thinking we had come all this way for a dead end and would have to turn all the way around to return to our cars.

Ralph placed one side of his face against the rock wall —first to his right then to his left.

I glanced behind me when a blast of wind caught my attention. When I turned around, I was swarmed in darkness, and he was gone.

"Ralph?" I called nervously.

"Through the gap, Blaire," he called out, his voice growing quieter.

When my eyes adjusted to the darkness, I leaned against the rock Ralph had been standing near with my right-hand side and gasped when I saw the soft yellow glow of Ralph's light deep within the narrow tunnel. I entered the gap between the two rock walls and followed. Wind blew through my hair, causing me to flinch as if attacked. I fumbled for my flashlight and switched it on again, scanning my surroundings with my little light. Nothing was near me; it must've just been the wind from the cave entrance. I sucked in a breath and marched forward.

We continued through the narrow tunnel until we reached an edge. Glancing at the alcove, I saw it was filled with fitted shelves and broken items. Whoever had been here had left in a hurry. Tables were knocked over, and scalpels littered the floor among the broken shards of glass. Three beds stood next to each other with the sheets half off. The expensive equipment was gone, suspiciously similar to the other room we had discovered in the mansion.

"Someone left in a hurry," Ralph said as he dropped a

step with a loud thump, then another until he reached the floor.

Once I was down, we searched the alcove. It had the entrance we had just come through and an exit in a dark corner toward the back. After searching what they had left in the room and finding nothing of importance, we entered the tunnel in the dark corner.

Beads of sweat peppered my forehead. I wiped it away with the hem of my shirt, but the shirt was already damp from my body; I was just wiping sweat over my sweaty face and not necessarily removing the sweat. I longed for a shower.

Soon after we entered the tunnel, it narrowed on us. Eventually, we were on all fours, crawling through it.

"I can't picture a bad monster crawling through this, like we're doing." I groaned as we moved forward.

"There must be other entrances, Blaire. We just need to find them," Ralph answered breathlessly.

"Yeah, or they used magic." My hands landed in mud, and I cringed. "Or our master vampire has a couple of Renfields to do the heavy lifting." I grunted, the air warmed around me, and my neck tingled. My heart beat so loud in my chest I suspected Ralph could hear it.

As if reading my mind, Ralph said, "Control your breathing. I know it's difficult for you, but try to relax. It looks as though the tunnel opens up ahead."

"Thank heavens. I don't think I can carry on in this tight space." Vivid memories of being stuck in my Ma's cupboard, my secret hiding place, for days until the neighbor opened for me surfaced to my consciousness. Scratching sounds behind me brought me from my memory, and I crawled faster to catch up with Ralph.

"What was that?" he asked nervously.

"I don't know, but fucking hurry." I bumped into his boot; my nail catching on his heel sent pain up my finger and arm.

The scratching neared me.

"Move!" I growled so he could go faster. I didn't know what was behind me, and I didn't want it to catch up to me either.

My left foot hooked on something, and I screamed.

Ralph turned that bright light in my direction, singeing my eyes.

I was temporarily blinded. My foot was still caught, and then something that felt like hard fingers grabbed my ankle. I screamed again, lifting my leg. I unhooked my foot from whatever it was stuck on and kicked at the thing. I connected with something, and it screeched. I pushed forward, bumping into Ralph again.

He moved faster as I crawled after him.

My fingers dug into the dirt as I navigated through the tunnel. I wasn't sure if my vision was still blinded from Ralph's flashlight, or if his large body had blocked all the light. All I saw was thick darkness and had to use the ground beneath me to find my way.

"I'm out. And another room is here," Ralph called out, his voice sounding distant.

"I can't see, Ralph," I said panicked as I felt my way through the darkness. Even though I was looking up, I still only saw black.

"I'll grab you when you come out," he called after me, and I followed the sound of his voice.

I crawled farther, then my right hand dipped into nothing.

Ralph grabbed me under my arms and lifted me, setting me onto the ground. The scratching continued as my vision finally returned in shades of gray. I could see an outline of Ralph as he pushed me to the side. I pressed my head against the cool wall of the cave and steadied myself against the cold rock.

Gunshots echoed.

I covered my ears as the pain stung. "Warn me next time, Ralph!"

"It was a mole-man." Ralph shuddered in disgust.

"I fucking hate those things!" I trembled just thinking about those hard, curvy fingers with its extra thumb and long nails wrapped around my ankle as it pulled my foot.

I blinked a few more times. My vision finally returned in full Technicolor.

Ralph held a long, skinny man with a fur-covered body and features similar to that of a mole, like a small human mashed together with a star-nosed mole. Ralph shot him in the head, but his star-nose was still on display, like a flower blossoming.

"I don't know why those things even exist. As if the mole animal isn't creepy enough on its own, they had to come in human size just to fuck with us some more."

"Me neither." Ralph threw the carcass to one side.

After that episode with freaky mole-man, I exhaled slowly, taking in our new surroundings. It was another room, another alcove, just as disturbing as the other; it too was trashed with the equipment removed. Something caught my eye. I went to pick it up.

"Don't!"

"Too late, it's in my hand."

"Now that we have established you're an idiot, what is it?"

"Curious, Ralph, I am curious." I punched him.

He faked how hurt he was and crashed to the floor.

"You need an Oscar, dude, seriously." I rolled my eyes. "It's someone's ring, like those high-powered men wear when they belong to a secret society. What could this one be? I've never seen it before."

The gold ring had platinum circling the red jewel in the middle. The jewel itself formed a unique pattern, like a curvy stick man with a line running through his middle.

"I don't recognize it either." The lines between Ralph's eyes deepened.

I tucked it into my pocket. "We can see if our search unveils anything when we get to your place."

"I doubt it, not if it's a secret society."

"Where is your optimism?"

"Back there with mole-man."

I burst out laughing. "Come, cry baby, let's get out of here. I've had enough of this place. It's giving me the creeps."

"Me too."

We searched for an exit but couldn't find one.

I stood with my hands on my hips and felt my frown deepen. "There's no exit. How can there be no exit? No one could have brought in all this equipment through that tiny tunnel we just crawled through. We barely made it through ourselves. They had to have used magic and a lot of it." I glanced up.

Ralph had been staring at me while I'd had my little tantrum and lifted his head the same time I did. It was still evening, so it was hard for us to know a large chunk of the roof was missing from the cave without the sun making it obvious. Twinkling stars waved at us through the natural hole in the mountain's side.

"Ladies first," Ralph said as he tugged on the rope he

had thrown up, ensuring it was stuck in place and could manage our weight.

With my backpack secured on my back, I grabbed the rope and started my ascent. My arms were shaking by the time I reached the top, then I felt the rope stiffen when Ralph started climbing.

By navigating through the various tunnels, we eventually ended up on the other side of the mountain. It faced the land where some of the were-animals had divided the forest into the various territories. Like the wheel of a bicycle, the walls that divided each were-animals territory was clearly visible.

Chapter Eleven

By the time we hiked around the mountain, up the various paths and around the rough terrain, we eventually found our vehicles when the sun greeted us with its smiling ray of kisses. I was too exhausted and grumpy to enjoy the warmth of the sun. My clothing was damp from the hike, and I knew I smelled like something awful and couldn't wait to hop in the shower.

"I'll pick you up around seven."

"Yeah sure," I mumbled as I climbed into my car.

We'd agreed we would check out the institute one last time. Whoever was taking the children—the were-babies—we suspected was gone. But we had to ensure they wouldn't return to take any more kids.

Ralph followed me to my house, then, when I parked in my driveway, he drove past, horn blaring and waving like a lunatic. He had way too much energy for someone who hadn't slept yet.

I entered my quiet house, my heart sinking to my toes at the realization I couldn't hear Scout's voice, her cries, or her babbling, as a two-year-old would when they had too much to say. I wiped my eyes dry, but then they burned. I ran to the bathroom and washed my face. My hands were dirty, and I had just smeared dirt into my eyes. Kicking off my shoes but keeping on my clothes, I climbed into the shower and put the water on full blast.

Finally, clean and smelling like my strawberries and cream, I pulled on underwear and a tank top then climbed into bed to sleep. Even though I was exhausted, our cave hike and staying awake all night was overstimulating my mind. I went from lying on my left side to my right side, then I lay on my back and stared at the ceiling. I climbed from my bed to search Scout's room and grabbed the little elephant she usually slept with, cursing myself for not packing it for her. But pleased at the same time because now I could sleep with it. With the plush toy tight against my chest and the smell of her easing my busy mind, for the first time since they had left, I allowed the sadness to overcome my concrete facade. The tears fell, that gut-wrenching feeling of loss and utter misery. And misery loves company, in my case, flurries of fucking anger—anger for allowing Demetri and his goons to force my hand. And now my baby girl was gone.

My only family.

Of flesh and blood.

Was.

Gone.

Eventually, when I was calmer and the tears dried, I finally drifted off to sleep. I had no dreams, but it felt like I had just closed my eyes, and then I was waking again. It wasn't so much the breathing that bothered me, but that it was by someone I hated. My jaw clenched as I grinded my teeth.

One man I loathed, apart from *he who had killed Ma*. Demetri's breathing was unmistakable, like the hairs in his nose played a tune. I jackknifed from bed to see him standing at the foot of the bed. Glancing at my phone, I saw I had only slept about three hours. I was still exhausted but seeing Demetri in my house gave me a shot of instant adrenaline, putting me on high alert.

"Wakey, wakey, sleepyhead," Demetri said, taunting me.

"How did you get in here?" I groaned.

Now we really needed to devise a plan where we could sleep undisturbed and not be found unless we wanted to. I would discuss my idea of installing a secret basement with Ralph tonight.

"Your door was unlocked," he said, pleased with himself.

Shit, I must've been too exhausted to lock the front door when I got home.

"Well, you're here now. What do you want?"

"You've hidden your little girl very well. My people can't track her or your pretty boyfriend."

"I told you, they were gone for good."

"That must hurt."

I won't cry, I chanted over and over. I won't let this man see my tears—even though he caused them—*again*. I ignored his question; instead, I stared at him deadpanned.

"Since I have nothing else to do, I thought I would pop by. I was here last night, but you were out. And, besides, Cleo wanted me to fetch you. She too is inquisitive as to which flavor animal you are. Unless you feel like shifting now so I can see—all of you." He licked his lips and, with his hands, outlined my body.

Ugh. So gross.

"At least get out, so I can dress."

"How do I know you won't escape?"

"Really? Out. Now." I pushed him out the room, closed the door and locked it.

Once dressed, I opened my bedroom door.

Demetri was waiting for me right outside the door. He pushed me against the wall, pressing his body against mine. "Let me see what we have here." He grunted near my ear, his warm sour breath against my neck.

I shuddered involuntarily.

With his chest still pressed against mine, his hands wandered down the sides of my body until he found the bulge of my gun. He *tsked* me, ripped open my jacket and removed my gun and two knives I kept sheathed in the holster. He continued searching by pressing his thick fingers around my thighs, moving down one leg then the other. He found my smaller spare gun in the ankle holster. He had commandeered all my physical weapons; I guess I would just have to use what was in my little treasure box of tricks.

"Now we can go." With one of his meaty hands against my back, he lightly pushed me toward the front door where one of the were-goons I had met at the wolf pack was waiting.

"We gots to go, D. We can't keep 'em waiting," Goon One said.

"Shut up." Demetri scowled then pushed me forward so hard I almost fell.

I sat between two large were-goon-wolves in the back seat of their Cadillac Escalade.

Demetri sat in front while Goon One drove.

"Where are we going?"

"You'll see soon enough," Demetri said without looking at me.

We rode for about an hour's drive out of town. I should

never have allowed him to take me, not that I had a choice in the matter. Rule one when a bad guy was involved: don't let him take you to another destination, because once you were in his car, chances of you escaping shrank down to next to zero. Sighing inwardly, I was a professional, and I had failed miserably.

Goon One took a left turn into the forest and stopped near an opening of an old mine shaft. We were on the far opposite side of the valley where Ralph and I had explored yesterday—or rather, early this morning.

Goon Two and Three opened their car doors with the one on my right motioning for me to follow him.

As I climbed out, something caught my attention when the boulder moved. The boulder neared, and I was momentarily frozen. I had only read up on them at school and again when I started at Ulysses.

"Hey, Zinjo, is the boss in or only Cleo?"

"Only Cleo is here," Zinjo replied clearly and so loudly his voice echoed off the surrounding trees.

The troll was massive. He was bigger than what I had studied in my schoolbooks. They needed to be updated. Zinjo was a dark green-brown color with four tusks protruding from his bottom lip, two on each side. The tusk on the outer side was large and the one beside it smaller. Even with those things against his lips, his speech was crisp and clear. He thumbed something, and it flared to life.

I flinched when he brought rags near the flame and lit his torch.

Glaring down at me, like I was dinner, he grunted. "Follow me."

When he turned, I noted the horns coming from his neck and down his spine. He reminded me of a dinosaur—

a talking, fucking Spinosaurus, aka spine lizard. One I was sure could squash me with a flick of the wrist.

Goon Two and Three were still behind me, ensuring I didn't bolt. Who did they think I was? I mean, I was good; I was fast, but I was outnumbered.

Demetri walked beside Zinjo with Goon One on the other side of him.

We entered the old mine shaft. Wet dirt and musk filled the surrounding air. The mine entrance began with high ceilings and wide-open spaces, but soon everyone had to move into a straight line, with Zinjo, the big fucking troll that he was, leading us down the shaft. I didn't think he could fit in that narrow tunnel, but he did.

We didn't walk for long and eventually stopped inside one of the rooms off the main path.

"Really, Demetri? Does it take all of you to walk a small woman in here?" a woman questioned when we entered.

"You can't trust this one, Cleo." Demetri thumbed in my direction.

"I want all of you outside, now."

"I was told never to leave you alone with her."

"Don't care. Now, get out."

"Cleo!"

"Fine. Zinjo can stay, but the wolves must get out."

"He won't be happy about that."

"I'll manage him. Take your pets out with you."

Once the goons and Demetri had left, only the three of us remained.

Cleo clutched my shoulders with her bony fingers. "We don't have time, Blaire," she whispered, her pearl blue eyes large and sparkly.

Zinjo moved to the other side of the wall then disappeared.

My eyes widened as I stared at her with a mouthful of teeth, trying to process what was happening. Eventually, I managed to mutter, "What's going on?"

"He must not get his hands on you." Cleo tugged me to follow her.

"He, who?"

"His name doesn't matter. It changes at his command."

I halted. "What the fuck is going on? Or you can forget about me going anywhere with you. I would rather take my chances with Demetri and his dogs than go anywhere with you. I don't know you."

She sighed. She was losing patience, but so was I.

"It's imperative he does not capture you or your daughter." Her gaze met mine, the intensity of her stare was not lost on me. She feared for my life. "This is what he does. He creates. He has the gift of life, but instead of using it for good, he's consumed by the lust of power it offers and the evil he can create." She swallowed, and it sounded like it hurt. She glanced over my shoulder, as if ensuring we were still alone. We were. "He has powerful people helping him. One can find true talents, except he couldn't pick up yours. Naturally, you intrigue him. It's only because of your connection to Demetri that he learned about you. And I've stalled him for as long as I can. But he doesn't know *everything*." That last word stung in the silence.

"But you do?"

She nodded. "Now come. We must go before they return." Cleo gripped my hand and pulled me toward the stone wall.

I braced for impact, but, instead of my face smacking against the rock, we walked through air, water, light? I couldn't be sure. When I opened my eyes, we were outside in the forest but not from where we had initially started.

The smell of rain was fresh in the air, with lightning cracking in the distance.

I turned back to see where we had just exited from. The room was still inside the mine shaft, but I saw a type of magical film that allowed light to refract so, I assumed, I saw what Cleo wanted me to see.

I moved my hand through the film. "Can they see us?"

"No. I opened the portal for only a short time. It should close soon." As she said it, the portal started to close.

I watched as the portal shrunk.

Demetri entered the room. His face paled when he realized we were no longer inside and threw items against the rock walls. The glass he had just picked up was about to go through the portal when it closed. For a second, I thought Demetri had seen me as he stared right at me. I could only hope I was wrong.

"Come. We must be quick." Cleo pulled hard on my hand.

Zinjo was out of sight. He was massive and hard to miss, yet I couldn't find the fucker.

I followed Cleo through the forest until we happened upon a door inside a giant sequoia tree.

She opened it, revealing a large room that branched into various hallways and other rooms with closed doors. "We're safe here for now. Give me a couple minutes to figure out a few things. I only planned to get you away from them, not what to do afterward." She sat on a chair and stared at me with pleading eyes.

"Thank you, Cleo." I sat beside her. "What you did must have cost you, but I cannot allow you to do any more. You cannot risk your life for me." I placed my hand over hers. "Now tell me. What is going on?"

Something more had to be happening than just a bad

man who was going all Frankenstein's monster in Sterling Meadow. And I suspected she knew a lot more than she admitted.

She shook her head.

"Tell me. How do you know about me?"

She exhaled a shaky breath, cleared her throat then finally answered.

Chapter Twelve

"One of the very first vampires to ever walk the earth created *him*, and they were turned by the father of them all. Therefore, *he* is powerful, a deity, one who is not so easily stopped." She paused to listen to the wind outside.

I listened as well. My saber ears prickled, but it was only wildlife and the storm clouds edging closer. No wolves were trying to blow down the house.

"Through the years, his power grew but so did his ego. He wants more. He wants to rule all creatures and monsters alike. Then he wants to dictate to the humans, to rule them all. He's drunk on his power, and it's blinding him." She rose and switched on her kettle. "Tea?" she asked, like it was a Sunday afternoon, and we were about to eat cucumber sandwiches and discuss the latest faerie fashions.

I wanted something stronger, but tea would suffice considering. "Yes, that would be great." I joined her in the tiny kitchen nook. It was so small that if I turned, I bumped into her. Even though the room was large enough, the kitchen only comprised a small portion of the space.

"He has been kidnapping specials, monsters, creatures—basically anybody with abilities. He has been testing on them, taking their blood and various tissue samples. Then, by splicing their DNA, he hopes to create his super soldiers. He grows the fetus in tubes, where he kills them and performs further testing while he perfects the specific DNA he needs. He has done this for years, and I suspect he'll continue until he has the right combination of DNA to create his ultimate monster. An army like no other."

"And you think this army will be indestructible?"

She nodded nervously. "I've seen the end result if he gets what he wants." She shook her head, like she was reliving a bad memory.

"You see the future?"

"Yes. I've seen multiple futures, but only one possibility could work. But only if you do what I tell you."

I didn't like the way she had said that. As if the future she saw rested on my shoulders alone. And if I didn't do what she said, it would end badly. I was terrified at the thought, but I had to know all of it. "Tell me."

"I know you're scared, and part of what I am about to tell you means you're pivotal to all our survival. And the only way to defeat him is to never get caught. *Ever*. He cannot lay a finger on you, never mind extract your blood. Or Scout's," she whispered. "Should he capture you and extract your DNA, understand you're the key to creating his ultimate monster. With you, he will be unstoppable."

"Shit, no pressure, right?" I said sarcastically.

"I'm sorry. I know it's hard to hear this, but you must *listen*." Her ice-blue eyes frosted a little more. The kettle had boiled, and she poured us tea and handed me a cup. "Stay hidden. Kill anyone who tries to hurt you. Kill them all. Start with that were-leopard."

Salvation

I frowned. I wasn't sure who she meant.

"The one who murdered your Ma."

I froze with the cup near my lips. "You know who he is?"

"I do, and, when you see him, do not hesitate. You understand? No hesitation. Ever. You need to kill him."

I nodded mechanically; my body numb. It would be my absolute pleasure to rid this world of that scum. "I've been looking forward to that day since I was eight."

"I know." She blew on the hot tea and sipped. "You'll tend to Demetri as well, so don't worry too much about him. Also, I know more, but, if I tell you too much, it'll alter your future. And that cannot happen. Therefore, I'll only provide you with enough clues for you to know when something awful will happen, to give you enough foresight to change the result to one that suits all our needs—the result you'll need to win, Blaire."

"Okay." I swallowed hard, and it hurt. My palms were sweating.

"But it won't happen now."

My frown deepened. "What do you mean? When will it then?"

"There'll come a time, after ten years, when you'll be tested at great lengths. Then, after Scout's thirteenth birthday, you will *remember* everything about our conversation from today. And it'll guide you to do what needs to be done."

I blinked back tears. This was too much. All of this couldn't solely rest on my shoulders alone. Surely? And that it would only happen after ten years sounded ridiculous. This information was scary enough. I doubted I would forget any of it.

"Do not fret, Blaire. You won't be alone. You'll have

powerful men at your side. They'll keep you out of harm's way and help you when the time comes."

I didn't trust my voice, so I just nodded.

"And you need to open your heart to them. These men will help you. Do not lock them out."

"I don't—"

She raised her hand to stop my words. "No! You have to let them in. Willingly embrace the love they offer. I know someone has hurt you, but they're important to your mission."

"Okay." I swallowed the words I had wanted to say. I'd never opened myself up completely to anyone after that man had murdered Ma. It was always important I kept my true self hidden. Not even Old Man knew everything about me. However, I had only loved one man before I had Scout.

Cleo had spoken little about Scout, only to say that after her thirteenth birthday I would remember. And I was concerned I wouldn't see her again. I had to know more about her. "Will I ever see Scout again?"

Her lips curled upward and reached her eyes. "Of course. You'll see her every year. Mason will keep her safe by protecting her with his life. Do not worry about them. He's the perfect protector. Another thing you have to promise me."

"What?" She had my attention now; I was hooked on her every word.

"Whenever they move and change their name, you have to write down the address and keep it in a safe deposit box."

My frown returned. That didn't make sense. "Why? Anyone can find the key, and then they'll know where they are. It's stupid to do that."

"You have to trust me, Blaire. Please promise me you'll do it. It's the only way. When you have the address, it's the step in the right direction you need to take. If you don't, we're all doomed."

"Shit, when you say it like that, of course I will." Something tugged on my chest, and it felt like butterflies had crashed into my ribs. This was all too much—the responsibility, losing Scout and Mason. Then Demetri and his goons were after me. I wiped away a lonely tear with the back of my hand.

A knock came on the door.

I froze, glancing in that direction.

Cleo patted my hand. "It's all right. It's only Raphael and Cofu," she said and opened the door.

A tiny knee-high gargoyle stood beside an eight-foot-tall giant.

"Come inside. Quickly."

Once they entered, Cleo introduced them to me. The gargoyle was Cofu and the giant Raphael.

The gargoyle spoke with a deep-centered voice that did not match his tiny cement frame. "She's pretty, Cleo. Can I keep her?" He approached me wearing a cheesy grin.

Cleo smirked. "No, Cofu. Don't bother her."

"Yeah, yeah. Is it because I'm short? You know you can't discriminate. Where I lack in stature, I make up in other places."

I giggled at him.

"At least I can make you smile, honey. You want to know what I can do with my fingers?"

"Cofu! That's enough. She's our guest, and we need to protect her, remember?"

"Pity. She sure is *purrrrdy*. Ooh, and that mouth."

"Stop it," Cleo chided and pushed him backward.

He stiffened and turned into his cement statue then re-morphed into a living, breathing creature. Neat.

"Fine. Just know, I'm good at what I do," he said with a raised eyebrow.

Raphael grunted, and Cofu's demeanor stilled.

"Enough, gargoyle," Raphael commanded. His voice sounded like thunder, deadly and penetrating. He extended his leather-covered hand to me.

I tentatively placed my hand in his and stared up at his black leather-masked face sewn together by silver thread, along with the rest of his armor. I couldn't see his face apart from his dark left eye; his gaze was intense and frightening. His mask was held together by straps sewn together and clips, with a mixture of hieroglyphics and something else I couldn't decipher written around the mask where his mouth should be. I was frozen in his shadow.

"Do not be afraid of me, little one," he said softly and sweetly, a contrast to his scary form.

The touch of his large, cold hand around mine took my mind off his scary eye and nerve-shattering voice. I didn't trust my voice to say anything. I could only stand and stare at him. He must've sensed my discomfort, because he rubbed my hand with both of his.

"I'm sorry I'm cold to the touch. That is not my doing. It is how I was created." It sounded like he smiled beneath his mask as he spoke, but I wasn't sure. "I'll protect you and your daughter with my life, but, understand this, when we see each other again from tomorrow onward, you need to ignore me. Make as if you do not know me. Understand?" He arched that one eyebrow.

"Okay," was all I could muster. I wasn't sure why or what he meant, but everything was happening so fast, and, at the same time, all I could do was listen.

"It's the only way you can stay safe. Nobody must know we're friendly."

I nodded.

"It's time," Cleo sounded, tearing me from my thoughts. "Demetri is coming."

"This way," Raphael said, pulling me toward a dark hallway.

Pounding started on the front door, followed by shouting.

The cold grip Raphael had on my hand tightened as he pulled me along.

I glanced behind me as they blasted the front door to smithereens. Wood splintered everywhere.

Demetri and his goons entered. His eyes met mine. "Cleo, stop! He'll kill you for this."

"Too late, Demetri, for I am already gone," Cleo said as she opened a door for us.

Raphael pulled me through the doorway while Cleo closed the door, but she was still on the other side.

"No!" I yelled after her, trying to break free from Raphael's grip.

"Keep moving, Blaire," Raphael ordered.

I turned to check where we were and observed an apartment in the city. I glanced at the door we had just come through to see it glow for a moment then wink out and resume being just another ordinary closet door.

"Whose apartment is this?"

"Mine," Cofu answered. "But we have to get out of here."

"Where are we going?" I asked, choking up. The events of the day were getting to me. Everything was happening too quickly.

Chapter Thirteen

Raphael drove a vehicle I didn't recognize, as it was custom-built to fit his large frame. I was speechless in the front seat while Cofu rambled about stuff I didn't care to listen to. My mind was still wrapped around the various places we had just travelled from and how we'd left behind the one person who could tell me more about my future; Cleo's magic had aided in our escape. We exited her place via a portal, but, instead of her joining us, she stayed behind to face Demetri and whoever their boss was. I had hoped she wasn't another casualty.

I was not fully aware of my surroundings. My head spun with everything Cleo had told me. Why me? Why now? What's next? How could I even possibly do what she said I would do?

And, whoever the man was, the one experimenting on the *specials*, he must never find me.

"Cleo said I had to bring you here," Raphael said as he parked his vehicle across the street from a building.

I glanced around. "Where are we?"

"The leopard's leap."

I hadn't recognized the building through my daze and confusion. My chest squeezed on my heart and lungs, and I struggled to inhale. Momentarily paralyzed by my fear, I caught glimpses of Ma's hand on the carpet, at her lifeless body. I was eight and in a secret closet, hiding from the man who had murdered her in cold blood. In my mind, I prayed he couldn't hear me, see me, or smell me. That miraculously, whoever had called him so they could leave, had inadvertently saved my life.

A hand grabbed mine, and I flinched. Staring into Raphael's one dark eye, I saw tenderness reflecting in that mysterious gaze. Perhaps Raphael really was on my side, even though he was employed by the man who could ultimately destroy so many lives.

"It's time, Blaire. He is here. Now is your *only* opportunity. This is the start of the events Cleo has put in motion for you."

I sucked in air. Exhaled. Stilled my screaming consciousness. I *had* to do this. I *would* do this. I *could* do this. Not just for me but for Ma and for all the times she suffered at his evil hands, all the times he had hurt her and me.

To cope with the mounting pressure, I went to my place, my dark place. It was somewhere I went to for my mind to focus on my target, to get the job done, to kill the monster. And he was the biggest one of them all, because he was my monster under the bed. And mine alone to destroy.

Grabbing my side, I realized Demetri had removed all my weapons, and I had nothing to defend myself with. Or to kill with.

"Here." Raphael offered a gun in his large gloved hand.

I smiled but knew it didn't reach my eyes. "Thanks."

"And take this just in case." He produced a large hunting knife.

I crossed the road fully armed and as ready as I would ever be and slipped through the open front door undetected. I listened for voices. Particularly *his* voice. Sounds came from one room to my left; I headed in that direction. I couldn't hesitate. I had to kill him. No thinking was allowed. I had to just do it. Now!

Guttural sounds escaped through a slightly ajar door. A female whimpered.

"Come with me, baby," he said in the throes of their wild lovemaking.

It was *him*, the shifter who had killed Ma. I could never forget that gruff voice for the rest of my life. I gently pushed the door open with my foot, ensuring it didn't make any sounds.

His body blocked the woman below him as he penetrated her.

My chest rose and fell. I needed to steady my breathing if I was to get this right. I couldn't make a mistake, or it would cost me my life. He was a were-leopard, and he was fast. Even though I was faster, I couldn't make any mistakes.

Aiming my gun at his head, I went to my dark place. I exhaled and fired.

Screams pierced the air. But I didn't see his body fall. His body was supposed to crash to the floor, but it didn't. He remained kneeling over the woman. Sweat dripped down the middle of my back. An ice-cold feeling engulfed me as panic rose within me.

I had missed!

Instead of falling, he rose from the bed, standing tall. The woman was still yelling; he backhanded her to shut her up, and then she lay quietly. She rubbed the cheek he had hit, her wide eyes penetrating mine. Blood dripped down one side of his face. I'd only grazed him. Shit. He turned and lunged toward me.

I fired again and hit his chest—one, two, three times.

But he kept coming at me and quickly.

I panicked. I wasn't supposed to panic. That was my only shot.

He hit me like a freight train, and we flew into a wall and then to the floor. The knife flew out my hand but I still gripped the gun. He straddled me with his hands and body pinning me. "Who are you?" he growled, spittle splashing over my face. "Who sent you?" His deep-set brown eyes searched mine for answers. He grabbed my head and slammed me into the floor.

Sparkly white stars flooded my vision.

"Tell me before I crush you with my bare hands."

Crying out was futile; he would kill me before I tried. I wanted to rub the ache at the back of my head, but he grabbed my wrists, forcing my arms to the sides and away from my body.

He stared at me with murderous intent. He was beyond pissed off. But then something happened; something snapped as recognition registered in his eyes. "Blaire? Is that really you? The little girl has finally grown up." He smirked. "Have you finally come for revenge? Little you, trying to hurt me?" He roared with laughter.

I froze beneath his grip. Everything depended on me not hesitating or allowing him the chance to escape. Time stood still, then, in slow motion, I moved my right hand that squeezed the handle of the gun. While he stared down at me, I moved the gun in his direction, undetected. I aimed the gun right and fired.

The bullet hit him in the side of his head. He fell backward and crashed to the floor. His wide eyes remained locked on me, like he was still trying to comprehend what had just happened. He was off me. And I was finally free from him.

The woman screamed again.

I aimed the gun at her. "Shut up, or I'll kill you too."

She did as I asked. Her body trembled as she nodded in agreement.

Like all horrors, he tried to sit up again. Soft flowing fur covered his arms then disappeared as if it had been blown away with the wind. His eyes glowed yellow then resumed its dark shade. A low guttural sound vibrated from his lips as his jaw morphed into his leopard jaw then into its human shape.

Even though the gun held silver bullets, it didn't slow him down with three bullets in his chest. Now that one was in his head, he was trying to shift into his beast, so he could heal himself. I had no idea he was *that* powerful. If he got it right and shifted, he would come after me again, and again, and hurt me worse than he had Ma.

I did what I had trained for all these years. I emptied the clip into his chest, leaving a hole where his heart should be.

He fell to the floor with a loud thump.

I kicked his feet for proof of life but there were none.

My chest rose and fell as I wiped sweat off the sides of my face. Even though I knew he was dead, I still watched him to ensure he had breathed his last breath. Then I noticed the chain around his neck, the one Dad had bought Ma before he had died. I'd looked everywhere for it when I had been helping Granny pack Ma's house after her funeral. He had taken it from her neck the day he had killed her. Bastard.

I ripped the chain from his neck and lifted it so the item

could fall through. I caught it and threw the chain on his body. I opened my hand to stare at the black orb as it changed colors—navy blue to green then red, purple, pink, orange, then slowly it became white.

Ma always told me I was *pure*, that my powers were *good*. And she always tested me with this orb. Smiling at the little item in my hand, a sense of accomplishment enveloped me with a renewed outlook. I could move forward now, no longer having to dwell on the past or on the man who had murdered my mother. Now I could look forward to what Cleo had said I was destined for, something far greater than revenge.

Something only I could do.

Chapter Fourteen

It felt so good to be in my bed, that sinking feeling as I finally relaxed coupled with the comfort of my soft mattress as it surrounded my aching muscles. I fell asleep quicker than usual, my adrenaline nosediving the moment I got home.

The events of my day were something to remember forever. I was finally content I had killed the man who had murdered Ma and had hurt me. Unfortunately—or fortunately, depending on who you asked—I didn't even know his name, nor did I care. The memory of his spark leaving his eyes when I obliterated his heart will stain me forever, but it was for the best. I wanted to remember that until the day I died.

But where there's a high, there's bound to be a low—of those no longer around. Raphael had confirmed with me when I got into his car that Demetri had killed Cleo. And her words clung to me like a vise—about the future, about my future, and how this so-called evil man should never catch me.

Raphael also mentioned a vampire named Noryx who acted as the big boss's go between. Nobody really knew who the evil boss was, except for Noryx. Raphael received all his orders from Noryx and hadn't been included in any of the inner circle dealings and would help me find Noryx to get to the big boss. Noryx was the one giving Demetri and everyone else orders that had been delegated from the man pulling the strings. Raphael also noted Noryx was something of an enigma with certain powers, and no one really knew how to contact him. He *always* contacted you.

Nonetheless, a smile played on my face as I thought about everything, and my mind finally drifted to sleep.

Something wet and slimy woke me from my slumber and moved against my cheek. Then a heaviness pressed against me. I opened my eyes and stared straight into Demetri's piercing gaze.

"My boss isn't too happy about what you have done, little girl." His breath smelled like dried blood; he must've just eaten.

I shuddered at the thought of him devouring a poor animal.

"First, you stick your nose where it doesn't belong, and now my boss has to go into hiding. Then you hide your daughter from us." He *tsked*. "And now, because of you, I had to kill Cleo, because she had sided with you."

"That was your choice to make, Demetri. You didn't have to kill her."

"Oh, I did, Blaire, and I can only imagine what she told you."

"Get off me, Demetri." I tried to throw him off, but he pinned my hands to my sides while his large body crushed mine.

He was still sitting on my lower body while he moved

over, placing a hand on either side of my head, and hovered closer to my face. "I was told to bring you to my boss's boss, but I thought I would have a little fun first." With one hand, he caressed the side of my face. "I can't resist the temptation." He came closer, licking the other cheek.

Ugh, all I wanted to do was wash my face and brush my teeth. Oh, and kill him.

"You smell like a dead animal," I groaned.

He chuckled. "I'm not hungry for food, but I am hungry for something a little tender, and possibly sweet." His hand trailed down my neck until his meaty fingers found my nightshirt.

Before he could grab anything delicate, a blur of black knocked Demetri off me, and they crashed into the opposite wall. Old Man hissed at the werewolf then bit into him before Demetri had time to react. Delicious sucking sounds emanated from the dark corner where they were, and I wanted to hurl. Old Man had his arms and legs wrapped around Demetri's body as his jaw latched onto his neck and sucked him dry, literally.

I wanted to bounce and clap, but I knew better. As much as Old Man enjoyed having an audience, this wasn't the time for childish behavior.

After a couple minutes of slurping and sucking sounds, only a leathery husk remained of the werewolf.

"Hmm, although he didn't look appetizing at first or wasn't my type, he certainly tasted delicious." Old Man licked blood from his long fingers.

"Why did you wait so long?" I crawled to the foot of the bed, closer to where Old Man cradled Demetri's corpse.

"I wanted him completely enthralled by you, my dear." He chuckled then grinned. Blood dripped down his chin and neck, staining his shirt. "You need to build yourself a safe space here. Perhaps a basement with a secret entrance."

I nodded and smiled. "I was thinking the exact same thing."

That thought recounted what Cleo had said, that some men would assist me—in ten years' time. If Old Man was still around and on my side, then maybe, just maybe, I could withstand anything that came my way.

"What the fuck, Blaire?" Ralph barged into my room, a gun in each hand and pointed at us. "What's going on here?"

"Is this your little boy partner?"

"Yes. Please be gentle. I like this one."

Old Man stood, dropping Demetri's corpse on the floor, and approached Ralph. "I won't hurt you, but no human is allowed to see me." Before Ralph could do anything, Old Man gripped Ralph's head and, with a penetrating gaze, put Ralph to sleep. "You'll forget you ever saw me, Ralph. Nod if you understand me."

Ralph nodded.

"Where is he?" Ralph yelled as he burst through the front door, gun pointing in my direction. It felt like deja vu, but Ralph's memory was scrambled, and I had to play the part.

"Who?" I asked, retrieving a second mug for him.

"Don't be coy. The bloodsucker."

"Oh, him? He's long gone, buddy."

"Fuck, Blaire. Why can't I meet him?"

"He's elusive. And he doesn't like other humans, especially when they run into my house with guns pointing everywhere."

"Fine." Grunting, he holstered his gun. "And the werewolf?"

"I was right. He paid me a visit earlier." I poured fresh coffee into our mugs and handed him one. "But Old Man got him for me."

"Blaire!" Ralph gave me stern eyes.

I shrugged and said as innocently as I could, "What?"

"Don't give me those puppy-dog eyes. You could've gotten hurt."

"I didn't, okay? I'm fine. And we got the fucker. The job is done."

"Just don't do it to me again. We're partners, through thick and thin."

I grinned at him.

"Where's the body?"

"Gone. Old Man said he'd take care of it for me."

Ralph sat on one stool near the kitchen island. "Now what?"

"We wait."

"Just like that?" Ralph asked, frowning.

"Just like that."

With hawk eyes, he watched me in disbelief.

"My intel has informed me the one performing those experiments has moved shop. And, from what I understand, he'll only return in a few years' time. We have to wait until then." My shoulders relaxed as I sipped my coffee, the hot sludge soothing my throat. I could feel Ralph's glare though, like a hot coal on my face. When I opened my eyes, his were penetrating mine. "Don't give me that look."

"What aren't you telling me?"

He was my best friend, but I couldn't tell him what had really happened. He couldn't know *that* about me, along with my abilities, let alone having friends in mystical places. And I couldn't tell him about my future and what I had to do to keep everyone safe. It was my cross to bear, and I would do so silently—until the time came, of course.

"Nothing, but what I want is to build secret basements in all our houses. Yours, mine, even Marcus's. I want each of our houses armed, with beds where we can stay should we need to. They must be impenetrable."

"Why?"

My smile reached my eyes. "I would rather be safe than sorry."

Chapter Fifteen

His warm fingers caressed my cheeks, wiping away the tears, and then he whispered, "Please don't cry, kitten."

"But you're leaving me. Again." More tears fell.

He pulled me into an embrace and held me close to his chest.

I wrapped my arms around his waist and held tightly. I heard the *duh-dum* of his heart; it was beating. He had told me it would only beat when I was around him, that somehow I always did that for his stone-cold heart.

"I have done what I can for now. But I'll return when you need me again. I promise you," Old Man said softly, gently, like one would for a child.

I pulled away from his body to stare up at him and frowned. "You knew before I explained it all to you?"

He nodded. "Not all. I only knew some of it." He moved stray hairs out my face. "I know what you're capable of, and I know that, in ten years, you'll need me again. And I'll be there for you."

"Why didn't you tell me?" More tears fell and stained his shirt.

"One cannot divulge the ending until the story has begun. And, as the little faerie had said, those of us who know the future cannot say too much to those who don't, for fear of failing and altering the course of our lives forever."

"I know." I nodded into his chest. "But you've only just returned to me. Mason and Scout are gone. You'll be gone. I won't have anyone else."

"Ralph will be there for you."

"He's my friend, and I work with him. But you're my family."

"Be strong, Blaire. You'll come through this a better person. And you *will* see Mason and Scout soon. I promise."

"But it's not the same as seeing them every day." I cried, swallowing the large lump in my throat. My face hurt from the crying, and my eyes were swollen.

"I know, kitten." He kissed the top of my head. "Believe me, I know." His voice sounded strained and full of sadness or regret.

"No, you can't possibly know what I'm enduring." I pushed him from me. "I have no one." A coldness flooded me.

Numbness.

My anger flared to life, like it had once all those years ago, before I knew about my saber, before I had turned into her. My anger was alive, bigger and scarier than ever and back from where I had kept it safely locked away.

No more nice Blaire; no more care Blaire.

No. More. Nice. Blaire.

Angry, bitchy Blaire was back.

"Just leave then, if that's what you want to do. Just go! Get out of my life. Again," I yelled, pushing him farther from me, and turned on my heels and stormed to my bedroom.

"Blaire?" he called after me, sounding tormented.

"No! Just leave me!" I slammed my bedroom door.

Through the door, I heard him whisper, "Love you, kitten, always and forever. And you'll see me again."

And then he was gone. Out of my life. Again. He always left when I needed him the most, torturing me with his tenderness and kindness only to leave me again. I couldn't handle it anymore.

My chest hurt as a piece of my heart broke.

A sinking feeling dragged me to my bed, and I fell on top of it. I was alone. My daughter was gone. Mason was gone. My parents had been dead for years. All I had was Old Man, but, even then, that wasn't often. He would only enter my life sporadically—when I needed him.

Perhaps he was right, and he would be there when the evil man returned to release his vileness upon Sterling Meadow. I had to have faith. But I was tired of getting hurt.

That was it, no more—my metal shields rose in double layers, with reinforcements around my heart, effectively locking myself away, leaving the hard mask behind.

Chapter Sixteen

"Are you ready?" Ralph asked. His hand rested on the door handle, as he was about to step out his car.

"Yeah, let's get this over and done with."

We crossed the parking lot toward the institute's entrance. The gate was locked, and the nurse at the station who would usually open it for us was absent.

"Hello?" I called into the foyer. If I only had human ears, I wouldn't have heard anything, but I don't, and I did. I turned to Ralph. "Let's check out back."

He nodded, and we walked around the side of the building. I heard noises and pulled my gun, and Ralph mirrored me. We crept alongside the dark wall. Screams pierced the night air, and we bolted toward them. I held my gun in front of me as Ralph ran beside me, both of us pointing our weapons ... at kids.

They had scattered large inflatable playhouses in the back area of the institute. One was a boxing ring, where the kids wore oversized gloves and tried to hit each other. The only thing they could hurt was themselves as they tried to lift the gloves, and their sides would hurt from all the laughter. They had filled another with water, where the kids were splashing and throwing a ball. They were swimming in this cool air, but who was I to judge? Kids didn't feel the cold, and they were were-animals; they felt nothing but heat. They welcomed a nice dip in a shallow pool.

I holstered my gun and stared at the festivities. When I saw Dr. Hilling approach us, we closed the gap and shook his hand.

"I'm so glad you decided not to shoot one of my kids," he teased. "Come, sit with me." He climbed the steps and sat on one chair.

I sat across from him while Ralph stood.

"I take it you haven't had any more abductions?"

"No, thank heavens. The two of you have done your job well. The kids and I thank you for your service, and I've sent the payment to Marcus." When he blinked, I saw that same slow motion where I could not avoid noticing his third eyelid slip across his eye and back again. It was both interesting and creepy.

I glanced at Ralph, who hadn't moved. I suspected were-animals still freaked him out a bit, even though we had been doing this for some time. But there's always a first at meeting a were-croc.

"We're happy that you're happy. I guess our job is done." I stood.

"Wait. I have a bonus for you." Dr. Hilling handed me an envelope. "It's just a small token of appreciation, to say thank you for putting the blackmailing culprit behind bars."

I peeked inside to see a few hundred-dollar bills. Score.

Ralph had located the person who had been blackmailing Dr. Hilling about the kids going missing. We had set a trap, had one of Ralph's cop buddies arrest him, and he would be serving five years behind bars. The judge had ordered monetary restitution to Dr. Hilling and the school.

Since we had stopped the kidnappings, the kids at the institute would be safe again.

I suspected Cleo had given the bad man a glimpse of his future, and he had moved away for a few years—ten to be exact—and only then would he return. I was sure he had enough DNA data to do his testing, or—which I hope would not happen—he would continue kidnapping specials but would test on them in a different town, location, or city. I wasn't sure, but I knew I would only see him again in a decade.

For now, we considered the case closed.

Part II

PRESENT DAY

Chapter Seventeen

I'd just finished my meeting with the Oracle, Lance's mother, who had informed me of my various gifts. Then, early the next morning, I had taken the first flight to Portland, Oregon. I'd memorized their address when I finally found the key and had opened my safe deposit box a few weeks ago. I had arranged for a rental car, which I collected after the plane landed, and drove straight to their address.

I parked across the street near their house, and waited patiently for someone to arrive. It was after 3 p.m. when a gaggle of kids were walking home from school. I sat upright when one kid broke away from the group, said *bye* and entered the house I was monitoring. It was Scout—a taller and much older Scout but no mistaking it was her.

I climbed out my rental, crossed the road and traversed the footpath. I honed in on that front door that had just closed, so much that I didn't see if anyone had followed me or was near the house.

As I was about to knock, someone cleared their throat. "Blaire?" a man said behind me.

I turned to face him. "Mason?" I blinked wide eyes at him.

His lips curled upward as he pulled me into an embrace. "It's so good to see you but you're early," he said into my neck and breathed me in.

That sent goosebumps throughout my body. I pulled away from him and stared up into his brown-green eyes. "A lot has happened, Mason."

The front door opened. I turned, and there she stood. Scout.

All it took was one *look*.

I glanced at the familiar green eyes, and everything came back to me. She was the key to my memory returning. It all hit me so quickly and hard that I stepped backward and had to lean against the side of the house in order not to fall over. The flood of memories hammered into me as I swayed back and forth, gritting my teeth as I remembered. One glance at my baby girl was all it took to snap my mind into place.

The green eyes I'd seen so many times in my mirror stared back at me. "Mom!" she cried out, wrapping her slender arms around me. She was no longer a baby; she was already my height at only thirteen, if not slightly taller. Slightly.

Tears streaked my face as I laughed, hugging her back.

"Okay, Mom, you can let go now. You're squishing me." She moaned but giggled at the same time.

"I'm sorry, it's just—" I wiped away tears. "I'm just so happy to see you, that's all."

"You saw us at the beginning of the year, Mom. You're carrying on like you haven't seen me in years," she said, still trying to escape my embrace.

Before I had arrived, I hadn't seen her in what felt like

ages. But the moment I saw her, all my memories returned. That's what I needed to unlock my mind—to lay my eyes on *her*.

Once a year, every year, in different locations throughout the country, we would all be together. And, as I had promised, once I knew of their new location, I wrote it down and placed it into my safe deposit box. And I had to do that because Cleo knew of my attack; she knew it would leave me with amnesia, and she made me promise I would do as she asked.

I had to experience all I'd been through the last seven months in order to meet Sebastian, Léon, and Salvador—*my Old Man*. No wonder the cheeky vampire would act strange whenever I was in his company. He wanted to see whether I remembered him. It was he who had been helping me—the strange keys, the locks, and erasing my digital footprints from the police records.

Warmth caressed my soul as I thought about the love and the newfound bond I shared with my new vampire family. They would be the ones to help me when the time came, to help me defeat that evil man—whenever he showed his face again.

When the time came, we would be ready.

My cellphone chimed again, but I ignored the missed calls and text messages I had received. All I could think of was my family. The rest of the world could wait.

Staring into my daughter's face, I was finally *home*. And I would give them my attention until such time when I had to leave.

Chapter Eighteen

The three of us sat for hours chatting. I told them everything that had happened to me these last seven months and omitted nothing. They stared at me with concerned expressions and sadness. But it was all forgotten once I had told them that just by being near them had helped me regain my memories.

I even told Mason about Sebastian. He took my hand and told me he understood. We didn't hold each other back in the love department, and I knew he'd had other partners throughout the years. But we shared our own special kind of love because of Scout and the dangerous situation we had found ourselves in—to protect the daughter we shared at all costs. And one of those costs had been our relationship.

The three of us spoke until the early hours of the morning. We made a family bed on the living room floor, so we could sleep together like we used to when Scout was a baby.

I woke to the smell of coffee brewing and Scout brushing her teeth. She was busy getting ready for school.

Salvation

My phone vibrated on the kitchen counter, but I ignored it as I watched Scout go from the bathroom to her bedroom, trying to finish.

"You need to answer your cell, Blaire," Mason said, taking mugs from the cupboard. "It's been ringing nonstop."

I sighed and stood from my comfortable bed to check my phone. It was Léon. He had left over a dozen voice mails and texts since yesterday. I suspected he would be angry after I had asked the pilot of his private plane to leave without me while I caught a flight here.

"It's Léon, I'm sure he's just worried about me. I'll take this outside." I headed through the front door and sat on the bench to return Léon's call.

He answered on the first ring and rambled in French—I suspected he was swearing at me—then eventually, he calmed down and switched to English. "Where are you? Are you okay?" His voice had lost its velvet touch. He was angry. He had never been this angry with me before.

"I'm sorry, Léon. I'm fine, I promise." I was still in two minds about telling him where I was. Somebody could be listening to our calls.

"I can't protect you if I don't know where you are," he complained.

"It's okay. I'm perfectly fine."

"When are you coming home?"

"Monday." I at least wanted to stay the weekend with Scout before heading *home* and before they changed their location again—which they did every year, and that time was nearing.

"Tell me which airport I can send my plane to fetch you from."

That brought a smile to my face. Did he think I would

reveal my location so easily? "Nice try, master vampire. I won't tell you. I'll buy a ticket and fly with the rest of the cattle in economy class."

He chuckled. His smooth caressing voice was sensual and seductive again. "I had to try." He sighed.

"What's wrong?"

"We've been looking for Sebastian and—"

"Did you find him?"

"No, but we will. Anne is adamant he's somewhere … near. Even our young Devan has channeled him. But, unfortunately, all we know is he's in the mountains."

"Which ones? Sterling Meadow is surrounded by them and the next towns."

He sighed again. "Lance has even offered to consult with the Oracle and will send word by tomorrow."

"Please keep in touch, Léon. I have to know where he is the moment you do."

The Oracle had told me that I would find Sebastian, but the time it was taking to get to him was stretching for too long.

"I will. And Blaire? You sure you're all right?"

"More than all right. Promise."

"Will you let me know where you've been once you get back?"

"Uh-huh." I smiled. I was sure he could hear how happy I was.

"Good." Then he was gone before I could say goodbye.

Ralph had also left a dozen messages when I didn't come home yesterday. Léon must've reached out to him and Devan when he realized it was only the pilot in the plane. I phoned Ralph to let him know I was fine, and we discussed what Léon had already mentioned about Devan sensing Sebastian still being alive. Although Devan picked up that he was not completely *well*, it also took a lot out of Devan to reach out to him and wasn't sure he could do it again.

"The boy was grey after he tried that stunt. It almost killed him," Ralph had said.

It was just the three of us, and we needed to take care of our own. Marcus was out of the picture completely, so we didn't care too much about what he did, nor did we inform him of our actions.

Ralph added that, apart from the continued searches, Ulysses was still doing well, and I had to come home to share the workload. He mentioned he and Devan would climb the Black Mountains that bordered Sterling Meadow and hike the town next door to see if they were at all near to where Sebastian could be trapped—or rather whether Devan could sense Sebastian better.

All this talk of mountain hiking in search of vampires reminded me of the time Ralph and I went hiking when we had been hunting for the monster who'd been taking the young were-kids from the institute.

Those memories hit me like a ten-ton truck. The children. Dr. Hilling. The baby vampire I had sucked the life from. It all came back. It was the same monster then who would be back for me now—if Cleo's premonition was correct.

A cold feeling washed over me as I remembered my time with Cleo, Cofu, and Raphael. Her words cut through me like a blade, reminding me to never get caught.

Then I thought of Demetri and shuddered—the werewolf who had hurt my aunt and had tried to get at me. But most importantly, I recounted the were-leopard who had killed Ma and how I had managed retribution. I recalled the leap and Sebastian and how I had seen *something* within him that reminded me of that man—and the anger that came with it—and I had exploded into my saber, that somehow Sebastian was connected to this man I had killed. Perhaps it was just that they were both were-leopards and metaphysically connected to each other. I had to understand more, but I couldn't let Sebastian know I had killed one of his own. I didn't want to know what Sebastian would think of me if he ever found out, and, what could be worse, it could've been someone important within the leap. I shuddered from the implications of my impending doom should any of it come out—if we ever found Sebastian.

"Would you like your coffee out here?" Mason asked, bringing me from my daydream and holding a cup of steaming coffee.

"Thank you." I took the mug and sipped—Heaven on my lips.

"Everything all right?"

I couldn't share some things with Mason, so I would seal those thoughts behind my shield. I would deal with them when we found Sebastian.

"Uh-huh. Hope you don't mind, but I'd like to stay here the weekend."

"You know you're always welcome here."

"I know, but it's polite to ask."

He frowned. "You must've knocked away half of your personality after that attack. You've never asked. You always bark orders."

I apologized and shrugged.

His lips curved upward and matched his smiling eyes—his age prominently showing at the corners. "I must admit, I love the new Blaire."

"Really? How so?"

"You are calmer, still kick-ass, but more ... relatable."

"I'll take that as a compliment." My smile mirrored his. "Would you like to sit down?"

"Nah, I just want to call in a sick day at work today, so we can hang out."

"I'd like that. What time does Scout get out from school?"

"Three."

Once Scout had left for school, Mason and I enjoyed a late breakfast at a coffee shop. He told me about the friends she had made and the boy who had caught her eye; he was a sweet fourteen-year-old who lived with his mom. Then he flittered over the few dates he'd had the past year without going into too much detail. Thank heavens. Those things, we didn't have to share.

"But they weren't you, Blaire," he said, his eyes penetrating mine.

Even though Mason and I were lovers and had raised a child together, I shifted uncomfortably in my chair under the weight of his gaze.

He pressed on when he realized I wouldn't say anything. "Scout and I have already discussed this, and I was going to tell you in three months' time when you were supposed to visit." He paused, sucking in air like it was his last, like he was afraid I would strip his head from his body. "We want to come home. We're done moving from one state to the next. We want to stay in one spot now and with you. Permanently."

"But you can't," I complained and sighed loudly. It was still unsafe. I didn't know when the proverbial shit would hit us in the face, and I needed to keep them safe until all that was finished.

"Yes, we can, and we will. You said it yourself, whoever

this monster is who wants us, you will fight him. And Scout is old enough now. She can help."

"No!" I folded my arms, shaking my head. "No," I said softer, gentler. "We haven't sacrificed so much to give her a life just to put her in harm's way again. No, Mason, I won't allow it."

"Her powers have grown, and she practices every day. She reads Nana's book every night and uses the wisdom within to guide her."

My head spun, but all I could do was stare at him. If my eyes could spit blades, he would bleed from a thousand cuts. I was shocked into silence. I pinched the bridge of my nose and finished the last of my coffee. "Mason—"

"No, Blaire, do *not* Mason me. I've done everything you've asked. Everything. Exactly as you asked. Your daughter needs to fly. Do not cut her wings before you have even given her the chance."

"She's thirteen. You can't expect her to do what I do."

"No, she doesn't have to do what you do. That's dangerous. But show her what it is you do. Let her learn. Teach her. You were fifteen when you started, and there's no better person to teach her than her own mother."

"When do you plan on moving back?"

"Perhaps we can come home with you?"

I rubbed my cheeks and dragged my fingers through my hair before tying it into a low ponytail. "You guys can come but only in three months' time. I don't want you before then. It'll be safer that way."

Mason's smile lifted his cheeks and brightened his face. He looked handsome, the man I had fallen in love with all those years ago. "That'll mean the world to her. Your daughter misses you. I don't think she can go another year without you."

Just what I needed, more guilt. But that wouldn't last. They would come home.

Chapter Nineteen

Mason and I spoke for hours while he drove around town, adding little bits of information about Scout I might like. "That's her dentist over there. She has her hair cut there. She and her friends always have ice cream over there on Friday evenings"—not today, they weren't. Today was all about us, our little family of three.

Mason parked his truck across the street from the school where we could wait the last five minutes before the bell sounded.

The bell rang, and Scout burst through the doors first and ran toward us, as if she had known where we had parked all along.

The idea that her own powers had grown throughout the years brought a smile to my face, but I tried not to linger. We needed to downplay her abilities. She had been shielding herself as hard as I did to mask her flavor from the metaphysical world, and, to her friends, she was only human. And if I had to be really honest with myself, her powers scared the living shit out of me. But I would be there to guide her, even though she had my mother's book —her Nana. I was the real deal and would be there for her.

"Did you guys hear?" Scout asked as she climbed into the truck behind my seat.

"What?"

"A fleshie is running rampant around town."

"A what?" I asked, frowning. I turned in my seat to see her face.

Her smile stretched from one ear to the other. "A flesh-eating zombie. A fleshie. Someone reanimated a corpse from a grave last night and didn't put him back. Can we go see? Please? Please, please, please …?"

I narrowed my eyes at her.

She raised her hands. "It wasn't me, I swear." Then she grinned.

I didn't trust that little sly grin of hers. "Can you put him back?"

She glanced at Mason then back at me and nodded. We could check it out. I didn't know if any assassins in Portland could put zombies back, but it couldn't hurt to try. No one wanted a flesh-eating zombie—*ah-hum*, a fleshie—chomping on humans.

"Fine, let's go. Where did you hear he was last seen?"

"Yay!" she said, clapping. "The last I heard he was at the old cemetery."

"Lone Fir?" Mason asked then eyed me. "Are you sure?"

"You said it yourself." I shrugged. "Who's better to teach my child than me?"

Scout cheered behind me.

We drove as fast as we could without breaking the law toward Lone Fir Cemetery, one of the oldest cemeteries in Portland. As we drove through the gates, we heard screeching tires as those visiting gravesites sped past us, trying to get out. Yep, we were in the right place.

"Okay, so zombies are not that common. Usually the undead kill necromancers before they can lead full lives. But some slip through the cracks and make money from it while they live in the shadows. And stay clear of vampires. But I have heard of a few who live with vampires. There aren't that many, but they're out there doing the vampires' bidding, usually to find important people or old money."

Vampires hated necromancers, because they could control the dead, and vampires were dead. Vampires feared them more than they hated them. But it didn't stop them from slaughtering all necromancers who crossed their paths. That was one reason we had to keep Scout safe. Necromancy was just one of her many gifts.

"Mason says you've been practicing," I said to Scout.

Her head bobbed up and down. "And I've been practicing on roadkill."

"Ugh, gross. I'm sure it smelt wonderful." I snickered at the thought.

"Yeah, it's not the greatest." She pulled up her nose in disgust.

Mason parked the car. As we were climbing out his truck, another car pulled behind us.

"The zombie is ours!" the man yelled as he climbed out his SUV.

His partner joined him, and they approached us like bats out a cave.

"We only want to observe." I raised my hands to show them my palms—a non-threatening stance.

The shorter of the two narrowed his brown beady eyes at us. "Fine, but maybe keep the kid in the car. This could get out of hand."

"No. I'm old enough to watch," Scout chimed.

I shushed her by placing a calming hand on her elbow, shaking my head. We didn't know who these men were or what they could do, and we had to be careful around them.

"Suite yourself. Just don't throw up near us, kid."

"I'm Blaire, that's Mason, and this is Scout." Perhaps if they knew our names, they would accommodate us and be friendlier.

The shorter one with the beady eyes responded, "I'm Butch, that's James."

"Stay out of our way," James reiterated.

"We will."

Argh, I wasn't looking forward to this at all. Who knew what these two assassins would or wouldn't do?

We followed them to what I assumed to be the central point of the cemetery.

"Can either of you tell me what happened that a flesh-eating zombie is walking around?"

"Who are you anyway?" James barked.

"Blaire. I work for Ulysses Assassins in Sterling Meadow."

Both men froze, turning to glare at me.

"The Blaire Thorne?" James asked.

I nodded.

"Holy shit! I can't believe it. Wait until I tell the boys that Blaire is on a hunt with us," James said, taking my hand in his meaty palms and shaking it rigorously.

My frown deepened. "How do you know who I am?"

"Who doesn't? Everybody knows how you slay the monsters. To say you're famous among us fellow assassins is an understatement."

I could only hope that was a good thing and that we weren't in any trouble because of my conduct. And from what I understood, the assassin profession was increasing as more creatures took to illegal behavior.

"Don't look so worried. It's a good thing. Promise." Butch smiled. His brown beady eyes softened around the edges. "Some of us have started a tally on the number of your kills."

"My what?"

"How many monsters you've killed. We hear it's at least two hundred."

"Wow, okay, but I don't think it's that many, unfortunately."

"Huh, okay. See? I *told* you." Butch shrugged at James.

"That means she's killed more," James said to his partner but loud enough for us to hear.

"Guys, I'm really not here to measure our di—" I remembered Scout was with us—"monster count," I added quickly.

"It's not only the count but your methods. You're notorious for your quick executions."

I groaned. I didn't want Scout to hear any of this. I glanced back at her, but she beamed at me, seemingly utterly proud.

"Great, guys. Thanks for the acknowledgment. But could you tell us what happened here?" I asked again as we came upon a body.

The fleshie—as per Scout's name for them—had taken a chunk from someone's neck who was still clutching a bouquet.

"There are two of them, unfortunately. The douche who did this didn't know what the hell he was doing and didn't return them to their graves. The one fleshie is Michael Dobbin. He was a former patient from Dr. Hawthorne's

Asylum. The other is Alice Merlotin. She was a well-known prostitute who was murdered just before Christmas. The forensics team removed her eyes, so they could see whether her eyeballs still held the image of her killer. Needless to say, they didn't, and they couldn't catch her killer." James informed us of this bit of information like we were on a tour of the graveyard. It was interesting though.

"Why did he do it?"

"This isn't the first time the douche has raised a zombie and didn't put him or her back. But it's rumored the deceased know who the robber was who stole money back in the early nineteen hundreds and hid it before they captured him. This asshole wants to know who that person was, so he can raise him as well for the location of the hidden treasure."

"This isn't the first time it's happened?"

"Nope," Butch answered as he felt the corpse's neck for a pulse.

I didn't need to touch her to know she was dead.

Someone started screaming.

Butch and James ran toward the screams while the three of us followed closely behind. We reached a large gravestone where the two fleshies were munching on another victim—who was now very dead. We grimaced at the sound of their mouths smacking together as they pulled the meat off the victims bones; they themselves hardly had any skin or lips, but the grinding of what was left of their teeth as they ripped off chunks nauseated me. The fleshies were too engrossed in their meals to hear Butch remove a large salt container from his backpack and pour a large circle around them.

"What are you doing?" I whispered, more for Scout's

education than mine. I knew what they had to do, but I wanted Scout to learn from them too.

"We have to lay a circle of salt around them to keep them inside, to use magic to control them and keep them from running away. Otherwise, they can continue with their killing spree," Butch whispered, closing the circle, then he muttered something that sounded like a chant in reverse.

Once done, the surrounding air seemed to snap, and something moved through us, similar to a breeze but not quite. But I knew it was his power. I glanced at Scout, and she was rubbing her arms, Mason not so much; he was a plain human and immune to magic.

Scout turned to stare at me, wide eyed, like a deer in headlights. I gave her the thumbs up, silently mouthing if she was okay.

She nodded and gave me a thumbs up in response. Good.

In a commanding voice, Butch said, "Your time has come to go back into the ground." He sliced his hand with a sharp knife, the blood dripping onto the grass within the circle. "With this blood offering, I release you back into your grave. Go now, and go in peace. Rest for all eternity."

The fleshies screeched, and they slowly sank into the soil. The ground shuddered beneath our feet as the fleshies bubbled, their corpselike skin turning into a frothing mess, and melting into the ground until they were gone, back with the salt of the earth.

Butch knelt onto the grass, wrapped his wound in a white cloth and said a prayer in another language I didn't recognize.

James collected the salt container and cleaned the knife before placing the contents into the bag it had originally come from.

Once Butch was finished praying, he stood, looking a little pale.

"Are you all right?" I asked.

"I'm fine. It takes a lot out of me to send them back," he said, but he was looking at Scout. "I sense she has the *gift*." He glanced at me when he said gift.

I had the gift too but only a smidge; Scout was the one who was blessed in its entirety. And it didn't help lying, because he knew; he sensed it. I nodded.

Butch pulled a blade from his bag.

My first reaction was to pull my gun and aim it at his face.

"It's okay," he said with a quiver in his tone. He was sensitive to my hostility, but I was only in mama-bear mode and protecting my cub. "I only want to offer her a gift. It was my first blade when I first started out. It brought me many years of good luck, and I hope it will do the same for her."

"Oh, I'm sorry." I holstered my gun but kept my hand on the grip.

Scout approached Butch and outstretched her hand.

"Here." He handed it to her, handle first. "It's nice and lightweight for you. The blade is clean but very sharp, and it's charmed. You know about all that? Why you need it charmed and how to charm your weapons?"

She nodded. "Yes. My mom has a book I've been studying. We say a specific prayer to charm our weapons, and we do it to protect our power and to keep the evil at bay."

Butch nodded, a thin smile playing on his face. "But nobody has shown you how to do it as yet?"

Her eyes flitted to me then back to Butch. "No," she whispered then played with the blade in her hands, rubbing the handle between her palms and pressing an index finger onto the sharp blade without drawing blood.

He smiled. "It's okay. I sense you're a natural." He touched her shoulder and closed his eyes.

The wind blew again, but it was warmer this time and not so intense.

"I understand why," Butch said and let his hand fall to his side. He opened his eyes, and they shone black with stars. "Stay hidden, little one. Don't move back home just yet."

His words sent shivers up my spine, and it felt like blades. I un-holstered my gun again and neared them.

When he stopped speaking, his eyes bled back to their darker brown.

"It's all right, miss," James reassured. "My Butch is a little eccentric. He doesn't always know what is normal to do around new people."

I didn't move away from them now that I was closer to Scout. I didn't want him to touch her again until I was sure he wouldn't hurt her. "What did you mean by that?"

Butch finally tore his gaze from Scout to stare at me. "You know why, Blaire. I won't repeat it. Those secrets are safe with me. I won't even tell James."

James huffed behind us, his feelings obviously a little hurt. I didn't care.

"No, James, it is not my secret to tell, only to reinforce," Butch said still staring at me. Then he whispered, "The time has come, Blaire. You need to return before they come for you here. Scout needs to stay hidden, or better yet, have Mason and her get out of town now. Don't wait for nightfall. You need to leave now."

Sweat dripped down my back, and the hairs on my arms prickled.

Mason shifted uncomfortably, rocking from one foot to the other.

I grabbed Scout's arm and pulled her closer to me.

"Perhaps we should leave now, Blaire. It's getting late," Mason said, nervousness evident in his voice.

The sun had already started to set, and the night was closing in on us.

"Listen to him. Leave, now!" Butch yelled then collapsed.

"What did you do to him?" James asked, lifting his friends head onto his lap.

"Nothing. We didn't do anything to him. Let's go, Mason." I tugged on his arm. "Come."

The three of us ran toward Mason's truck. My lungs burned as we sprinted. When we reached the truck, we piled in, and Mason floored the gas.

"We need to pack," Mason said.

"Mom, what's happening?" Scout asked, tears streaking her face.

"It's okay, baby girl. It'll be okay. You and Mason need to pack and leave, and I'll go back to Sterling Meadow."

"But why? You've only just arrived."

"Somehow this Butch guy saw what you are and, in doing so, saw the evil who has been after us for years and after you since you were a baby. And it's time. The event we've been planning for all these years is about to happen now." The back of my throat hurt as I swallowed. I won't cry. I couldn't cry in front of Scout. I didn't want to freak her out more than she already was. I had to be strong, the backbone of our little family.

Mason was in shock as he drove in autopilot to his house.

Once inside their house, they packed what they could while I packed my one bag.

It felt like I was reliving that day when Demetri had first followed Mason. I had packed their bags, gave him all my money and had sent them on their way. It was happening all over again. And it was my fault. Again. I should never have returned. But if I didn't, my memory wouldn't have returned.

They were ready and waiting at the front door; we had to say our final goodbyes.

Scout was crying, her eyes swollen and chest heaving.

I pulled her into an embrace, and I held her as tightly as I could. I closed my eyes, my aura flared to life, and I pushed a little of it into her, just enough to offer her the strength she needed to move forward. Without me. Again. To remain hidden for a little while longer. She could do it; she was old enough to understand.

"I love you, Mom."

"I love you too, baby girl." I kissed her forehead. "Now go with Mason." I stared at him and nodded that I was ready to let go. They had to leave.

Mason kissed my temple, grabbed Scout's hand and pulled her from me. The memory too painful to bare, again.

"I'll send word in three months' time, Blaire."

"You know how," I said and tried to smile.

As they pulled out of the driveway, the flood works came, and I couldn't stop them this time. I cried until my body ached, and no more tears remained. I washed my face, pinched my cheeks for some color and called a cab.

Chapter Twenty

The moon was at its highest when I knocked on the Labyrinth side door. One guard I'd never seen before opened it and asked what I wanted. I explained who I was and that I needed to see Léon urgently. He took my bag and dropped it inside and escorted me through the maze of the place. We walked through the storeroom where all the liquor was kept and through another door that exits near the bar area for the nightclub, *Kiss*.

Warm bodies packed the venue, the lights were dim, and everybody fixated on one man alone.

Léon's hands cupped a woman's face. He leaned forward to kiss her, stopped and stared at me.

My breath caught as his dark gaze turned into something else, contracting my body in fearful pleasure.

Léon moved one hand to grip the woman's neck while the other squeezed her waist. Instead of his usual delectable kiss, like I had witnessed before, he showed his fangs and bit on her tender flesh, all the while maintaining his piercing gaze on me.

The crowd roared to life with an applause fit for a superstar; women and men cheered at the delicious sight. Moans of sensual satisfaction surrounded me, which made me realize why this place, *Kiss*, was always full every Friday and Saturday night. Something happened here nobody else could offer, that only one man could—or rather a vampire named Léon could.

Without realizing, my fingers caressed my lips, remembering what his mouth could do—the kiss we shared not that long ago. I wanted to turn and flee; it had been a bad decision to come here. I should've gone straight home, but I knew Léon would want to see me. And me being here would only end in a delectable disaster I wasn't sure I could crawl back from—especially with Sebastian still missing.

Léon abruptly released his smiling victim as one guard dragged her to the couch against the side to recover. In a blink of an eye, he was right in front of me.

The guard who had brought me here stayed beside me until Léon waved him away with a swift flick of the wrist. The guard pouted and exited through the door we had just used.

Everybody on the dance floor stared at us, but soon they were blanked out as my vision tunneled until all I saw was Léon.

"Something happened, didn't it?" he asked tenderly, his smooth voice like velvet caressing my skin.

I shuddered in desirable confusion. I didn't trust my voice; I nodded, blinking back tears. My emotions were still raw from seeing Scout and the memories that had followed, kicking me in the gut, and the harsh reality of the evil about to be released upon us, causing Scout and Mason to flee yet again. And now Léon—the brother of the man I had shared my heart with was before me—offered me a world full of desire.

I was a complete mess.

"Come," he said, gripping my elbow as we headed back the way I had come but headed toward his office instead of into the Labyrinth. He let go of my elbow, and his hand moved to the small of my back as we entered the office.

Heat penetrated my lower back from his fingers, sending a tingling sensation up my spine. I had to avoid his contact if I wanted to stay sane.

"Sit and tell me what's got you rattled." His voice caressed my neck and swirled around me, easing my nerves —but only slightly, because heat was creeping up my face and between my legs.

"I saw her," I mumbled, yet flustered.

"Who?" He sat beside me on the couch and leaned an arm against the back of the couch with his hand resting on my shoulder.

Warmth travelled from his hand and through me. His touch was meant to comfort me; instead, it was loaded with sexual fulfillment. I had to stop thinking selfishly. I had just messed things up with Scout *again*, and here I was thinking of myself and the man in front of me.

Tears fell as I thought of Scout.

He faced me, placing a bent leg on the couch, and moved closer until that knee rested on my thigh.

I turned to face him.

"Speak to me, Blaire. What happened?" His velvety tone soothed my nerves.

I leaned forward so our faces were inches apart and whispered, "I found Scout. That's where I've been. I had to see her, Léon. I had to find my little girl."

"Is she hurt?" he asked with love, his expression genuine.

I shook my head.

"No, but something happened …?"

I told him about the zombies and the two assassins who were there, about the things Butch had said about Scout and advising us to leave, that the evil was coming.

Léon edged on nearer, his knee still resting on my leg, but he pulled me in closer. Cupping my face in his hands, and, in that smooth voice, he said, "It wasn't your fault. You're safe, and you're home, with me. And Mason is keeping Scout safe. You can relax now. Breathe."

I nodded. I knew he was right, but it was all too much. But it was comforting sitting there with him, to share my heartache with someone I had considered a close friend.

Léon's one hand caressed my cheek with his face close to mine.

I focused on his lips, licking my own. As much as I knew I had to pull away, I didn't want to. I couldn't. I wanted him. I closed my eyes when our lips touched—his soft lips against mine. I opened my mouth to offer myself to him, his tongue tangling with mine. I placed my hands over his, entwining our fingers, and brought his hands into my lap. Pulling away from his embrace was like throwing ice over my hot body, and I wanted more of that heat, his ocean-blue eyes calling after me.

Léon stared at me, waiting for me to make the move, to get farther away from him.

But I didn't move away, and he didn't either, even though I sensed he wanted to. It was wrong. But it was also right. I climbed onto his lap.

He leaned backward until his head rested on the armrest.

My fingers were still entwined with his.

He moved our hands until we were cupping my ass and pulled me in closer until I felt his hard body beneath mine.

Letting his hands go, I placed mine on either side of his head and leaned forward until my lips were on his again for a brief kiss.

His hands moved up my shirt and lifted it off. Then he kissed along my neck, tentatively seeking that pulse vampires craved.

"Do it," I said huskily. I wanted to feel what it felt like to be *his*, to be bitten by him, by someone whose touch can wield unrestrained passion.

He opened his mouth against the pulse in my neck and bit. His sharp fangs entered me, and his hands pulled me closer.

Heat exploded through me as my body wanted to melt into his. I was like soft clay in his hands. The heat through his full lips and sharp fangs sent erotic shivers down my spine.

He moaned against my throat, and I grinded my hips against his. He tugged on my pants, ripping them apart until only the thin material of my panties remained between us. His hand moved between my thighs and under my panties and rubbed on my soft, delicate folds.

I moaned against his ear as he bit harder on my neck, making me writhe with another intense orgasm. As I rode the wave of his pleasure, he pushed a finger inside and played in my delicate depths, rubbing against that sweet spot that caused wave after wave to crash into me, until I was spent. I collapsed on top of his chest, out of breath.

Léon gently removed his fangs; it felt like butterfly wings flapping in the nape of my neck. He applied some pressure and kissed the bite wound. "You were wonderful. And you taste"—he licked his lips — "utterly delicious."

I was too weak to move from his chest, but I giggled. "Yeah, you aren't too bad yourself, vampire."

He huffed. "Not too bad? Is that all?"

I laughed again. "No, you were ..." I swallowed in anticipation. "Orgasmic."

He chuckled and kissed the top of my head. "But I'm not done with you yet, *ma chérie*."

That caught my attention. I lifted my head to meet his eyes. But before I could do anything, he had flipped me, I was on the bottom and he on top, naked and positioned between my legs. He had stripped off his clothing in that nanosecond while he had flipped me. I was too shocked at that quick movement to even burst out laughing from being love-drunk.

He hovered above me, waiting for me to say *yes* or to push him away. I knew I had to say *no*; I knew I had to push him away. But I didn't want to. I wanted him inside me; I wanted him to touch me, all of me. I closed my eyes and nodded.

He pushed the tip inside and waited until I opened my eyes again. "Look at me, Blaire. I've been waiting patiently for months for this. I want you to enjoy the look on my face, as I yours."

"Okay," I said and felt my cheeks flush.

Then he released his passionate wrath upon my body. The time he had spent not giving into his own desires poured over us and in me over and over again as he found his rhythm.

My whole body appreciated his and vibrated with each of his powerful and calculated thrusts. I moaned as the next orgasm hit, my fingernails digging into his back, and I was sure I drew blood. My enjoyment triggered his orgasm.

He stiffened for a second and then pounded harder and faster into me without restraint. He pulled back his head and grunted in sexual satisfaction and released himself within me.

I cried out in pleasure as I climaxed in carnal gratification, my body squeezing around his.

He collapsed on top of me, sweat blending us together.

I held him close to me. I felt the *duh-dum* of his heart, the strong rhythm of it pounding against my chest.

"Only you can make my heartbeat like that, *ma chérie*. Only *you*." He lazily lifted his head. The look in his eyes told me what his heart couldn't. "It's always been you, Blaire." He kissed my temple and slowly sat up, bringing me with him so that I sat across his lap again. "I didn't want to say anything, but I cannot, and I will not remain silent any longer. I love you."

My throat closed up from his confession. I wrapped my arms around him and embraced him. "I don't know what to do anymore. How can I love you and Sebastian?"

"Easy. When Sebastian is back home, we take it one day at a time."

"I feel like such a hussy."

He chuckled. "Hussy? Huh?"

I hit his chest. "You know what I mean."

"*Ma chérie*, nobody will think anything less of you. Your heart has been locked away for so long that it has so much room in there for love that you don't know what to do with it. And nobody will love you more than Sebastian and me."

"You make it sound romantic."

"That's 'cause I am." He pressed me against his chest

and held me there, his soothing voice caressing my skin and sending sensual goosebumps everywhere.

He held me in his embrace for a while, as if he sensed I needed his closeness. I didn't feel the cool air until he let go and pulled me to my feet to follow him to a bathroom around the corner, so we could clean up. In comfortable silence, he opened the shower, testing the water before I joined him. He added some liquid French soap to a sponge and rubbed soap suds all over my body as delicately as possible before cleaning himself. Then, when he was done, we rinsed, and he dried me first.

I watched in awe at how this master vampire cared for me, with so much love behind each of his delicate caresses. How had I not seen *him*, the sensitive man behind the dark shadow of a vampire? My heart wanted to burst with happiness—and cringe and die on the floor for what we had just done.

The betrayal, how could I live with myself?

Once we were dry, he grabbed one robe from behind the bathroom door and wrapped me in it. It reached the floor it was so big, but at least I was clothed. We sat on the couch again in comfortable silence for a few moments.

"I have men going out every day and night to canvass the mountains. We will find Sebastian and bring him home." When a tear fell, he wiped it away with a tender finger. "Please do not cry—unless they're tears filled with happiness?"

"They're both." My smile faltered at the sides.

I heard a knock on the door, and then it opened before waiting for Léon to answer. Salvador glided in, like he was floating on water. "I would ask what is going on, but I can see the afterglow on both of your faces and know it went very well." He grinned.

He was just the Old Man I wanted to see. I knew he still thought I didn't have my memories back yet and so did Léon. Perhaps I could play with Salvador for a bit, just to see his reaction. I stood and stalked Salvador like a predator.

He backed up until he hit the wall with a loud thump and, with panic etched in his words, asked, "Blaire, what are you doing?"

I remained silent as I raised my hands to touch his face, but he grabbed my wrists before I could; he was keeping me away from him. "Is this not what you want? You see the look in Léon's eyes, and you crave the same look?"

"Uh, no, Blaire. It's not like that."

"Blaire?" Léon questioned, but I ignored him; this would be epic.

"What? Am I not attractive enough for you, Salvador?"

"You are beautiful, but …"

"But what?" I stared into his glacial eyes. "Old Man."

Realization flickered in his eyes upon hearing my name for him, and he grinned. "You remember?"

Laughing, I backed away from him. "Yes, and you should've seen the look on your face."

"What's going on?" Léon asked, slightly confused by our banter.

Salvador brought an arm around my shoulders and pulled me into a sideways hug. "I missed you, kitten. I'm elated to have you back."

"*Kitten?*" Léon questioned.

"Your father and my mother were close when I was young. Didn't he ever tell you?"

Deep lines appeared on Léon's face. "No? When, Father? You never mentioned any of this to us."

"I was her protector. She was my kitten to take care of."

"And when she had amnesia, why weren't you there to protect her?"

"That, my son, was something she had to endure, so she could be part of your and Sebastian's lives."

"What aren't you telling me?"

"We'll have to band together, my son, and fight. I've notified the council of the impending doom that will soon be upon us. Now that Kitten has regained her memory, she'll know what to do."

I grinned up at him, my arms still wrapped around his slender waist. His heart too had started to beat once I lay my head against the side of his ribs.

"Ah, and there it is. Like music to my ears."

"You too?" Léon asked, shocked upon hearing his father's heartbeat also.

"Yes. She's the only one who can do that. And the love you feel for her is pure and unmatched."

More tears fell that I didn't have enough dry fingers to wipe away.

"And now? Why the tears?"

"I'm happy. I really am happy."

Chapter Twenty-One

I had fallen asleep beside Léon and slept in his embrace until he awoke me around 4 p.m. I'd slept for so long my head felt groggy, and my limbs were stiff and not working so well. I must have been more exhausted than I had thought.

We planned to search for Sebastian during the night, so Léon could join us.

As I stretched, Léon pulled me in closer and planted butterfly kisses along my neck and down my chest. He sucked on a nipple and bit down.

"Owe!" I cried out mockingly.

He sucked until he left his mark. "There, now you're mine."

"And Sebastian's."

He sighed. "Yes, yes. And Sebastian's." He chuckled then moved to the other breast and did the same.

Now both breasts had love bites. If I was still in school, that would've been funny. But as an adult, it was just so childish, but it felt great.

My cellphone rang, the tune alerting me that it was Ralph.

"They're coming with us this evening?" I asked Léon.

"Correct. They're probably waiting for us outside."

"Hi, Ralph," I answered.

"Help!"

"What's wrong?" I asked, panic laced in my question.

"Gargoyles, at least ten of them. Get your ass out here and help us."

"Shit, okay. Where are you?"

Ralph gave me the address, then I ended the call. As I turned to Léon to tell him what was happening, he was already heading to the bathroom.

"No need to say anything. I heard it all. Come, my little love button. I've always wanted to rescue a male assassin." He smirked. "How do you think Ralph will repay me?" he joked, licking his lips.

I threw a pillow at his head, which he caught before it could hit him.

"Don't hold your breath, vampire boy."

"Vampire *man*!"

Once we were dressed and heading out to Ralph and the rabid gargoyles, Jean-René caught us before we could leave and insisted on joining us. When he saw us, with Léon's arm draped over my shoulders, he raised an eyebrow in disapproval.

I felt scrutinized under his gaze. As if I was the one to seduce Léon, *as if*. I smiled sincerely at him, even though I felt like punching the grimace from his face.

"What is this, Léon?" He had waved an accusatory hand in our direction.

"One cannot stop the heart from wanting a little more, dear friend."

Salvation

"I of all people know that, Léon. Your brother isn't even cold, and she has latched onto you."

Léon glared at his friend with such hostility I thought I'd hate to be the recipient of those dagger eyes.

"Please forgive me, Master. It's just—"

"Do not raise the issue again, Jean-René. I won't tolerate another outburst. We've spoken about this before." Those disapproving daggers were still out and had just drawn first blood.

Jean-René seemed to have physically shrunk an inch or two as he accepted his master's command and groveled for his master's forgiveness.

"You can stay, Léon. Marc and Sawyer are with me," I muttered, pushing myself away from him.

"No!"

I froze mid-step.

He pulled me back into his embrace. "I'm not hiding my love for you anymore. The sooner everybody knows about us, the easier everything will go." Then he turned to his friend. "You know I'll always love you but not in the way you so desperately crave. I can never be enough for you." With his free hand, he pulled Jean-René toward his body and whispered into his ear—it sounded like his words were in seductive French.

"Allow me to join you, as a way to ask for your forgiveness," Jean-René said, staring at me. "I'll assist in ridding the gargoyles."

Jean-René sat in front with Léon while I was squished between my two bodyguards. As we neared the address Ralph had given me, something flew into the Jeep, and it swayed. Sawyer and Marc climbed out first, followed by the three of us.

The gargoyle laid on the ground near my feet; its concrete head had split in two upon impact.

I saw Ralph and Devan each fighting at least four of the stony critters, with one on each of their legs, and laughed; it looked like they were fighting toys. "Can these things do any real damage?"

"No," Sawyer answered while backhanding one that flew at him. "They're like overgrown ants with small bites."

Léon opened the back of the Jeep. We all grabbed our choice of weapon—mine was a baseball bat.

One flew at me, and I struck it, launching it in the direction it had just come from, and it turned to stone before it shattered upon impact on the ground.

Léon and Jean-René had their own flavor of vampire power as they played with the attacking gargoyles. Jean-René forcefully turned them into stone while Léon swung powerful bursts of air at them, popping them into a cloud of dust.

Sawyer would bite into them with his sharp teeth and rip their heads from their bodies before they could turn to stone. His way was a little gross, the gut-wrenching sound of blood and guts spewing everywhere and down the front of his shirt. Marc's way was gentler. He twisted their bodies in the opposite direction to their heads, severing the spines cleanly, while I played ball with their bodies.

Soon the gargoyles were dead, shattered, or had decided they'd had enough and ran away.

Ralph and Devan looked spent as they approached us. Scratch marks and bites covered both of them, their hair sticking out in different directions.

"Are you guys okay?" I asked between bouts of giggles. "What even happened out here tonight?"

Ralph and Devan sat on the sidewalk, their tired eyes staring up at us. "The little fuckers ambushed us," Ralph answered.

I shrugged. "Why? They rarely attack first, unless provoked." I narrowed my eyes.

"They were pissed that we killed their leader."

"Oh shit, yeah, that should do it then."

All the guys burst out laughing, and the sounds of their warm chuckles were wonderful. But then something tugged on my chest, and guilt reared its ugly head—survivor's guilt, one couldn't be happy, one needed to suffer in silence for a certain amount of time while mourning. And twelve hours hadn't been long enough after saying goodbye to Scout. I still had a few more hours of misery to go.

"It was an accident. We were just driving. We didn't see it," Devan admitted.

"This is gargoyle territory. What were you guys doing here anyway?" Léon asked with a smile still playing on his face.

I was glad I wasn't the only one who thought this was amusing.

"I was teaching Devan how to drive, and he took a few wrong turns. It was an innocent mistake." He shrugged those large shoulders in defeat.

Everybody burst out laughing again; even Ralph and Devan joined this time.

After a few moments of laughter and happy tears streaking my face, the moment sobered us up, and we collectively realized what we had to do next—search for Sebastian.

Ralph cleared his throat. He and Devan stood, and

Léon finally broke the silence. "We have an hour's drive ahead of us. My guys have searched all the mountains near here. Now we have to branch out a bit."

All heads nodded in agreement.

"Ralph, do you remember when we had that case up at Lake Hills Institute?" I asked.

"You remember?" He gasped.

I nodded and gave him a quick rundown about seeing Scout and how my memory had returned.

He pulled me into a hard bear squeeze, knocking out my breath. After a few seconds, he finally let go. "Yeah, what about it?"

"I was thinking whether anyone searched those mountains yet."

I watched his face as he remembered the events that had taken place over ten years ago. He glanced at Léon then back at me and shook his head.

"Perhaps we should start there, the mansion, the institute, then the mountain," I suggested.

Ralph nodded. "Yeah, it's a little out of the way, but it's a good idea. We should definitely check it out now."

Chapter Twenty-Two

We stopped at the crumbling mansion first, since it was on our way to the institute anyway, and before we would attempt a search through the mountain Ralph and I had hiked ten years before. The mansion still sat roofless, with more of the paint peeled from the walls, and the door was now lying on the floor with the rest of the debris. As we had done before, we went into the basement to see if the place still looked like a crazy scientist was blowing up shit.

We found shelves ripped from the walls, a broken gurney, and a thick layer of dust blanketing everything. It was safe to assume nobody had been here in a very long time. After testing shelves against walls and dragging desks into the middle of the room, we found no secret passages leading us anywhere. It was just four walls below an old house slowly falling apart.

We piled into the car, but, before Léon could pull away, I told him to stop. "You guys go ahead. I want to walk to the institute."

"No!" Léon scolded, shaking his head. "You will not go out there alone. I'll walk with you."

I didn't want him to, but I knew he wouldn't allow me to go on my own either.

"We'll wait for you guys at the institute. I wonder whether Dr. Hilling is still around," Ralph said, pondering the thought.

"No idea, but if he is there, tell him I'm on my way." I winked wickedly.

"Nah. I want to see his expression when he sees you come around the corner." Ralph chuckled.

"Yeah, your idea is much better." I cackled.

Dr. Hilling hadn't been very fond of me, as I had always pissed him off somehow. I wondered whether he still felt the same way. But that thought would have to wait. Right now, I had things to do.

Ralph waved us off as he pulled his old vehicle onto the road and drove away.

Jean-René moved into the driver's seat, gave me a stinky glare and followed Ralph.

I didn't know why Jean-René had it in for me, but again, it was a problem for another time. I had a problem right now as I stared at Léon. He wasn't aware of the *real* me, the *real* Blaire, and all my little boxes of magic tricks.

"Uh … Léon? You need to know something about me."

His gaze pierced my soul. It didn't help my situation, but I needed to tell him.

"Tell me everything. I want to know all that is you."

"Right." I paused, contemplating the best way to say it. "Just understand, you might not like this about me."

"It takes a lot to scare me away. Don't be coy."

"I warned you," I advised and undressed.

His dark gaze nervously glanced around us, trying to see

if another soul was in the area. "You kinky minx you," he grunted and undid a button.

"No! Not you, just me. And watch."

He stopped undressing and stared wide-eyed at me. Then a mischievously grin splashed across his face as I stood naked before him. "Ooh, *ma chérie*."

"It's not what you think, dirty, filthy vampire."

He licked his lips and flashed his fangs.

I grinned then started my change. The other were-animals I had collected retreated into their caves as my saber emerged. She was much larger than them and would be the only one I would ever change into. She charged at me. Bones snapped, tendons pulled and stretched. With a burst of white light, I turned into my very large saber.

Léon mumbled things rapidly in French I could only assume were swear words. "*Ma chérie!* What is this?" He raised his hands at me, shock evidently splashed all over his cold demeanor.

Through sharp teeth, I replied, "This is who I really am. Even though I hold other lycanthropy strains, my saber is my *true animal*, the only animal I will ever shift into." I growled, scent marking him.

He rubbed behind my ears, petting me like one would a kitten. "Stunning!"

"I want to canvass the area. You can either stay here and wait for me to return or fly while I run. We can search the forest together, cut the time in half."

He nodded and levitated, so he could get a bird's-eye view, while I sprinted deep into the forest.

While I searched the forest floor, something pressed on me. I couldn't feel any magic or power directly around me as I ran, but I sensed something there. Without having to see where he was, I could *feel* Léon wasn't too far from me. Then, from instinct, I glanced up.

Léon stared down at me, the weight of his glare cocooning me. We had somehow formed a metaphysical bond of our own, whereby I could sense his location. It was a strange feeling, something similar to my connection with Sebastian before it had been severed but not quite the same.

Finally, I reached an area that seemed to have housed someone once upon a time after our first search of the forest but had left long ago. The little wooden house was crumbling as roots from neighboring trees had grown through the wooden walls and was slowly pulling them to the ground. The roof had collapsed within the broken walls, and debris lay everywhere. I immediately thought of "Hansel and Gretel" and shook the horrific story from my head.

Apart from the eerie dwelling, the forest was just that. There were no hidden doors, holes, or vampires lurking behind trees. There was nothing. No trolls, faeries, or fay. Once I was content no monsters were hiding in the forest, I returned to where I had stashed my clothes and shifted into my human form and dressed. Glancing at the night sky, I noticed Léon standing high on a tree branch, staring at me with unknown intent. Once I was fully dressed, I headed in the direction of the institute.

A whoosh of air pushed past me then in front of me. And Léon leaned against a tree up ahead.

I smiled at him and stopped right before him.

The line of his body touched mine. He bent down and kissed gently. "You are so easy to love. You are courageous, powerful, and a force all on your own."

My cheeks flushed at the compliment. Wrapping my

arms around his waist and pressing my ear to his chest, I heard his heart thump.

He gave a long sigh as he relaxed in my arms and kissed my temple.

"You're not so bad yourself, vampire, but only once you let people inside." I glanced into his deep-blue eyes, the dark gaze I always seemed to get lost in. Now I couldn't wait to fall instead of always trying to stop myself.

"Hold on." He held me tightly, and we glided skyward.

I clung to him so fiercely I thought I would pass out—then I remembered I needed to breathe or I would pass out.

He stopped midair. "Open your eyes."

I did and gasped, squeezing him tighter. I saw the city lights ahead of us, the sky with the natural lights twinkling above us, and the dark shadows of the forest below us. The mountain to my left stood eerily concealed in the twilight. That was the mountain Ralph and I had searched all those years ago where we had found remnants of a scientific lab.

We hovered in the air until something knocked me from Léon's embrace, and I plummeted. The air whipped at my face as I fell, and the ground inched closer toward me. I had about five seconds before I would become animal fodder.

Léon yelled as he fought with a dark blur that had been so stealthy that Léon hadn't heard him fly near us and knocked me from his embrace.

I tucked my knees to my chest and braced for sudden impact. This would hurt. Slowly, I opened one eye, watching the ground get closer.

Then something hit my side, knocking the wind from my lungs, and we flew into the sky again. My stomach bubbled with the sudden movement. All I saw was the stars as they neared. When I blinked, we were inside a cave, as if we had magically flown through a portal.

The person carrying me slowly lowered me to the ground, and, when I could stand unaided, he let go of me.

"Thank you, Noryx," a familiar voice sounded from somewhere within the cave.

I turned toward that voice I had heard before and squinted in the dim light. "Shannon?" My stomach sank an inch. I had met Shannon at a dinner party where he was the host and campaigning to be the first monster in politics. He wanted to be Governor of Sterling Meadow.

One blink and the blond-haired man was before me. I had to stop blinking; these vampires were faster than the speed of light. I felt my frown deepen, and that familiar tinge of anger I usually kept locked away rose to the surface. It had been him all along.

The shock of this revelation was like a punch in the gut —betrayal of his own kind and of Léon's friendship.

"Now, now, Blaire. Don't think about it, or I'll hurt your lover boy," he said, oozing with smug confidence, then grinned.

I wanted to wipe that smile off his face.

"Where is he?" I asked, panicked.

"He's safe for now. But, before you can see him, I need to know who else is here."

I pursed my lips.

Shannon edged closer to me, gripped both shoulders and shook. "Tell me now, or I'll hurt your boyfriend." He pressed his fingernails into my arms until blood pooled around the tips. "Don't test me. I'm not in a good mood today."

"Fine! Ralph and Léon are with me."

"Léon? Really? I'm amazed he didn't send his dogs instead." He released his grip and paced, tapping a long thin finger on his bottom lip. "*Hmmm*, I would have to think hard about how to handle him. Where is he now?"

I shrugged. "One of your men was fighting with him."

"Ah, that must be why one of my soldiers hasn't returned as yet." Shannon glided to Noryx and whispered near his ear.

The other vampire disappeared into thin air.

"He can teleport, in case you were wondering."

No wonder neither Léon nor I had heard him when he hit us.

The stare I gave Shannon was not my friendliest. I knew it would enrage Léon when he found out his friend was the one behind *everything*.

"You cannot hurt me with your stares, little one. Léon maybe, but we shall see what I do with him."

Movement caught my eye when a dark figure entered the alcove. His face was hidden behind a leather mask with only a dark penetrating left eye to guide him. Raphael. Our eyes met, then he broke contact first as he stood before his master.

"Raphael, just the monster I need." I didn't think Raphael enjoyed that particular reference. "Take Miss Thorne to Sebastian. But I forbid her to touch him. You understand? I don't want him healed by accident."

Raphael nodded, gripped my arm and pulled me behind him.

Chapter Twenty-Three

I followed Raphael through the mountainous passageways. I didn't recognize the room we were in as one of the rooms Ralph and I had discovered all those years ago. My memory was back, and it was still in tip-top shape, even though it had been on hiatus for months. That room I had just been in and this passage I was walking down was all new. Either we were in another mountain, or there was more than one way to get in and out of this chunk of rock.

"I remember," I whispered so only my captor could hear.

He stopped and placed his large thick finger against his mask where I assumed his mouth was meant to be, showing I shouldn't talk about it again. I wasn't sure if he was just a giant underneath all that leather or if he was Frankenstein's monster. Either way, he was big and on my side.

Now I understood why Raphael had glared at me at Shannon's monster dinner and how he had made me recoil. But he was trying to see whether I recognized him, which I didn't—not at that time. I was sure all the monsters had known about my ordeal, and he wanted to find out if I knew him.

I nodded my understanding to remain silent about our partnership, and we continued forth.

After a few minutes, we entered a dark room. Raphael flicked something in his hand, and a flame came to life, which he used to light the torches that hung against the walls. The dim lights revealed a cowering body inside a cage made with a certain type of hard metal.

"Sebastian ..." My throat closed up as I tried to swallow my tears; I couldn't finish my sentence.

On the ground sat a malnourished man, his spine and ribs showing through thin, dirty skin. His hair was greasy and brown, not its shiny or blond natural state. It had only been two weeks.

Two.

Weeks.

Yet Sebastian looked like someone who had been starved for years. His head moved painfully slow, so he could face me.

I ran to his cage and fell hard against the ground. My knees hit the rock painfully hard, but I didn't care. I would survive that. By now, tears streaked my face as I stared into his gaunt face; dirt caked his naked, emaciated body.

"What did he do to you?" My eyes were misty as I pushed my hand through the bars to touch him.

He recoiled as if I had hurt him.

"Sebastian?"

His usual bright green eyes were dark and haunting; that golden sliver dull. He shuffled all the way to the back of the cage. Something sizzled. Sebastian howled in pain and moved from the bars.

Glancing at his cage, I noticed it wasn't just silver. I

leaned to get a closer view and saw the metal move with green and red slivers of something. I wasn't sure what it was made from, but it certainly was detrimental to Sebastian. He could usually touch metal, but this stuff seemed deadly to him, burning his skin when he touched it.

Raphael patted my shoulder, and I flinched. "Give him time. Much has happened."

I rose and pounded on Raphael's chest. "What did he do to him? Tell me now."

Raphael gripped my hands, so I would stop hitting him, and held me still. "You know what Shannon has been doing? Cleo told you what he was capable of ten years ago, or have you forgotten?"

"No!"

"And when he saw his window of opportunity, when Sebastian was at his weakest, he took him."

"What do you mean by that?" I leered into that one eye. Then it dawned on me. "Was I his weakness?"

He nodded.

The tightness in my chest returned, squeezing my heart at what I had done. It was my fault.

I stepped away from Raphael, pulling my hands free from his grip, and spied Sebastian's wide eyes.

He cleared his throat as if he had just woken from a bad dream, and it sounded like he had scraped chunks of his flesh. "Blaire?"

"Yes, Sebastian." I choked back tears.

"Is it really you? I thought you were dead," he whimpered.

I fell to my knees again, with both my arms through the bars this time. I needed to touch him. "As I did you. But I'm fine, and I'll get you out of here." One hand touched his face, and he leaned into it while my other hand rested on his shoulder.

His one hand cupped the hand on his cheek. He took my hand, smelled my palm and kissed it. His hard lips pressed gently into my hand.

"What did he do to you?" It broke my heart to see him in such a state—weak, emaciated, and half the man he used to be. I wanted to rip Shannon's head from his shoulders for doing this to him. I had to help Sebastian. "Come closer to me. Let me try to help you."

He realized what I wanted to do and shook his head. "No. Don't touch me, not here. I will only weaken you."

"I don't care. Now let me help you," I growled, my hurt and frustration evident.

He pushed away my hands and moved to the farthest part of the cage where I heard a sizzling sound again then smelled burning flesh.

I pulled my hands back out. "Move away from the bars. The cage is burning you!"

"Do not help me. Promise me. You have to get out of here and save yourself. Please. He cannot capture you too." His eyes flitted from me to Raphael. He did not know Raphael was on my side, but we couldn't share that with him or risk Raphael getting killed himself. We needed to keep him on the inside.

A blast of power erupted in the room, and the air shifted. Noryx appeared before me. "Shannon wants you back." He and Raphael shared a look, then he disappeared again.

"Next time he does that, I'll rip out his fucking throat." I glowered at the spot where he had just been standing. With tenderness in my eyes, I turned to Sebastian. "I need to go and see what he wants, but I'll return, and we are getting you out of here."

Raphael pulled my arm.

I stood and followed him to where we had just come from.

Once we were back in the same large room I had first entered, I gasped for air as I stared at Léon. They had strung him upside down, with blood pouring from a neck wound.

His haunting gaze piercing mine.

Léon blurred at the sides as my pulse thundered. As if taking away one man from me wasn't enough, Shannon had to take Léon too; although I didn't think Shannon knew what Léon meant to me. Perhaps if he did know, he might kill Léon sooner. I couldn't have that. I couldn't lose both of them when I had just found them. Do I save one at the risk of losing the other? If I saved one and Shannon found out, would he kill all of us quicker? I needed to find a way out of this, a way to get the men I loved to safety.

As my breathing steadied, I focused on my surroundings to see what had happened to him. They had bound his arms behind his back, and some wire—so thin it looked breakable—was twisted around his torso. Yet it kept him from freeing himself. Léon was a powerful vampire. He wasn't someone who was easily caught, strung up and left to bleed to death. That wire must be made of the same material as Sebastian's cage.

I didn't know how I would get us out of here on my own, but I had to think of something and quickly before one of them succumbed to their wounds. Swallowing the large lump in my throat, I ran toward Léon, screaming. I yanked that wire, and large hands pulled me away and into their embrace.

Salvation

"Let go of me, Shannon."

"Struggle against me, and I will kill him." He glanced at the vampire whom he had once considered a friend. "I'm sorry, dear friend, but you're in my way."

Léon hissed then swore at him in French.

Shannon *tsked*. "Your words mean me no harm." He chuckled. "As you can see, one of my inventions has improved somewhat." He waved a bony hand in Léon's direction. "That not even you, the great Léon, Master Vampire of Sterling Meadow, can break free of its hold."

"Watch your back, fledgling." Léon grunted. "One's secrets always have a way of coming out."

"You don't scare me anymore, *master*," he spat and tightened his grip on me.

Immediately, I stopped and went limp in his arms. I had to do what he asked. I had no choice.

Shannon set me on the ground and sat beside me.

Léon watched me, us, his pale expression faltering at his usual sharp demeanor.

"Now, where were we?" Shannon asked, forcing my attention to him and loosening his grip. He was a little too happy for my liking, tapping a finger on his lips.

I moved as hard and fast as I could and backhanded him in the face.

Someone flew into me, and we crashed into the wall behind me, hitting my head hard against the stone. He pushed me against the rock, one hand around my throat while the other dug a thumb into my abdomen; I could only assume was to bruise an organ. And it hurt like a motherfucker.

"This is my first soldier, Blaire. Please say *hi*."

"Fuck you."

Soldier Boy squeezed my throat until specs of stars

clouded my vision, then he relaxed a bit. "Apologize to Shannon," Soldier Boy said through gritted teeth, spittle hitting me in the face.

"Let go of me, monster toy." I wiped my face dry with a free hand while the other gripped Soldier Boy's wrist, a failed attempt at keeping his hand from crushing my larynx.

"Release her," Shannon commanded, and Soldier Boy obliged. "You really don't want to fight us, Blaire, not when you're on your own." He waved a manicured hand around and in Léon's general direction, knowing full well nobody would help me.

I eyed Raphael, but that stoic man kept watch on Soldier Boy and Shannon, not wanting to risk our private partnership.

Léon moved, and I glanced in his direction.

Shannon rubbed the side of his face I had just smacked. "First off, welcome to my new lab. I was chased from my previous ones a few years ago and had to make new ones." He thumbed a golden ring adorned with a red ruby in the middle on his long finger. It reminded me of the one Ralph and I had found in one alcove in this mountain. "And I've been waiting patiently to have you with me, Blaire." His words dripped with venom.

"Is this what you've been doing with your talents? It was you all along."

"Yes, biding my time until I had perfected them." Shannon put an arm around Soldier Boy's shoulders. "Beautiful, isn't he? He's only one of them. There are more."

I regarded Soldier Boy properly for the first time since he knocked into me; he was flawless. Nothing was out of place or skewed or misaligned. His muscular body hummed with power. "Too perfect maybe." Even his short raven hair was perfect, not a strand out of place. His eyes were dark and soulless. "But can he sing?"

Shannon grunted at my uncouth comments then pressed on with a smug expression as if I hadn't said anything. "He was the first of many I've created, and together they'll join the squad who'll be tasked with protecting Sterling Meadow."

"The humans won't allow him." I jerked my chin in Soldier Boy's direction.

"Oh, but they will. You don't know how convincing I can be."

From the corner of my eye, Léon moved again. Blood had stopped dripping from the neck wound, and he had somehow managed to stand without alerting them to the fact. Thank heavens he was a little more powerful than I had thought, otherwise he would've been a drained and mummified master vampire of nothing.

Raphael had moved closer to Shannon, blocking everyone's view of Léon, which I assumed was a strategic move.

"Your soldiers are complete. What'll you do now?"

"Well, as perfect as they are"—Shannon ran a hand over Soldier Boy's delicate features; he was a little too pretty for my taste—"they could always improve. And that's where you come in, my dear. Since I couldn't get your daughter, you'll have to do. And I would've had you sooner, but Kasdeya fucked me over, and Simon was greedy. So I had to finish it all on my own."

I had reached my tipping point; too much had happened, and I needed a break from these monsters. My anger boiled to the surface, and, for once, I welcomed it with open arms. The glow started at my feet, like it always did, and my vision clouded as if fog had entered the room.

Shannon glanced down, and his eyes widened. "What the—"

My anger flared to life with a white explosion, without me changing into my saber. I blasted Shannon and his soldier to the other side of the cave while Noryx disappeared into thin air—*chicken shit.*

Raphael stood steadfast, like the impenetrable monster I knew. He had blocked the blast from hitting Léon.

Shannon remained unaffected by my little display of chaos and grabbed me.

I froze.

He grinned.

I tried pushing him from me, but he didn't budge.

"Not so fast, Blaire. I was surprised by your little display of power just now, and it makes me very excited to have you."

"Let go of me," I said, struggling in his grasp.

"No." He leaned forward and whispered, "You are mine."

I had to get away from him and soon. Glancing over Shannon's shoulder, I saw Léon motioning for me to get away from Shannon. I didn't know what he wanted to do, but I knew we had to get away from Shannon somehow, grab Sebastian and get the hell out of here. It wasn't too much we had to do—*yeah right.*

But then, I noticed Léon seemed weak as he hung over a chair that kept him upright and was paler than usual. I doubted he could do much, let alone get all three of us out of here in one piece. The blood loss he had suffered and whatever that wire was they had wrapped around him had weakened him into his current state. It was up to me to do something and quickly.

I wasn't sure whether I could duplicate that white explosion, so I lowered my shields. Perhaps I had a party trick in my little treasure chest. I dug inside and grabbed the first thing I could find. I gripped Shannon's forearms.

He grunted in surprise.

I let the power run amok over the vampire.

Shannon fell to his knees, screaming and scratching.

"Now!" I yelled.

We only had a small window of opportunity before Shannon would realize the fire ants and wasps were all a figment of his—*ah-hum*—my imagination. Yeah, a faerie had given me that sweet trick.

Raphael ran toward Léon and pulled him to me, so we could escape. When I had Léon's hand in mine, Raphael pointed to the stone hallway and whispered, "Go the way we came and collect Sebastian on your way out. I'll take care of Shannon, to give you enough time to escape." Raphael pushed us toward the passageway.

My explosion of anger from earlier had caused some rocks to fall, so we had to climb over a few boulders as we headed toward the room that held Sebastian. The ground shook from a late aftershock, and more rocks fell, blocking the passageway from where we had just come. It would take Shannon a while to get through it, unless Noryx returned.

Léon's one arm was around my shoulders as I kept him upright, and we walked the cave passage. He tripped, and we both fell. Hard. Climbing to my feet and pulling Léon to his, I noticed his eyes were hooded, his mouth gaped open, and his tone paler than usual, even though his neck wound had healed. He was struggling to walk from losing so much blood, making it hard for me to keep him and myself walking upright.

Fatigue was hitting me just as hard, and I wasn't sure I could keep going. I still couldn't believe how Shannon had somehow subdued and drained most of his blood and almost killed him. I was half carrying him, which was slowing us down considerably. And we still needed to find a way out of the mountain. I didn't know what other tricks Shannon had up his sleeves and only hoped Raphael would keep Shannon and Soldier Boy contained long enough for us to get to freedom—safely. But until then, we both needed to keep going but faster. I was steadily losing ground as I carried the vampire.

It wouldn't help anyone if both of us were too exhausted to continue. He was stronger and more powerful than me and could carry me for longer, but not the other way around. I stopped us from walking, placed my hands on Léon's shoulders and stared into his deep-blue eyes.

"This isn't working, Léon. We're both on the verge of collapsing. I suggest one of us gets up our strength. I need food, a full-body massage, and twenty-four-hours sleep. All you need is blood to recover. So I'm offering myself to you. Drink." I craned my neck toward him.

"All I heard was a full-body massage," he said with a lustful smirk.

I gently smacked his shoulder. "Of course, that's all you heard."

Léon chuckled, then his eyes glistened at the thought of what I had just offered him. He gently pushed me against the cave passage wall and bit in one swift motion.

It didn't hurt, but it sent tingling sensations throughout my body as I draped my arms around his neck and enjoyed the sensation of pleasure during this time of devastation and need. I didn't even feel guilty. I welcomed the jolt of excitement and almost cried out in disappointment when he pulled away and applied pressure to stop the wound from bleeding.

Salvation

He stood back, staring at me with dark eyes filled with stars and rosy cheeks. He was well fed. "Thank you." He kissed me chastely. "Now let's find my brother and get out of here." He grinned mischievously, knowing what he had just done to my body. He was pulling my hand now and running.

I smiled to myself and was glad I could assist, even if it left me slightly shaky.

We finally entered the room where Sebastian was being held hostage, and he was still cowering in the cage's corner. The smell of burned flesh was still fresh in the air. I knew one of his powers was he could melt metal, but I didn't think he had the strength to walk, let alone use any of his powers.

Léon hissed when he saw his brother, swore in French then told me to stand back. He did something with the lock on the cage with enough power that it rained like confetti all over me—it felt like insect bites.

I pulled up my sleeves to see I had tiny red welts covering my forearms.

Léon kicked the cage with a booted foot, opening the lock, and pulled his brother to freedom. With one arm around Sebastian's waist, he half carried his brother—now we were ready to leave.

We ran farther down the passage until we reached a fork. We opted to go left and hoped it was correct. We didn't have a lot of time; either of Shannon's monsters would be on us if we didn't get into the open soon.

When a cool breeze caressed my hot and sticky skin, I breathed a sigh of relief as the evening sky greeted us. We finally exited the mountain. First glancing around to ensure no monsters were lurking in the dark, we continued running. I took Sebastian on the other side, and we both carried him. By working together, we could cover more ground and quicker. I had no idea where we were, but we continued running through the forest, following the moon.

No monsters were anywhere, and I was grateful for that. My foot caught on a root, and I fell, bringing Sebastian and Léon to the ground with me. Léon hoisted Sebastian first, with them trying to pull me to my feet. When I was finally standing, I hooked my arm around Sebastian's waist again, and we continued walking. It was at a much slower pace this time, but we were still moving. We stepped over a fallen tree, and my foot caught on a small branch sticking out, and I fell again, knees first.

"I can't anymore, Léon." I shook my head, still on the wet grass on all fours.

Sebastian sat on the fallen tree and reached for my hand. Léon sat beside Sebastian while I sat at his feet with my head resting against his knee. I needed a few minutes before I could attempt standing to sit on the tree beside them.

"I'll go up and see where we are. Stay here," Léon said, standing.

"Don't worry. I ain't going anywhere."

With those parting words, Léon was up and gone. A few short seconds later, he returned. "Noryx is on the other side of the mountain, searching for us. If we're to avoid him seeing us, we need to go to the left and stay near trees. He can't see us if we do that. Ralph and Jean-René are waiting for us near the institute. When we're closer, I'll leave you again and fetch Jean-René. He can fly and help us with Sebastian."

I nodded; the thought of finding Sebastian and getting us out of here gave me the strength to push forward. I didn't think I could go very far, but I would try. We had to.

"Can you call Jean-René using your telepathic vampire channel?" My question dripped with sarcasm.

"I'm still very weak, Blaire, but I can try."

My shoulders sagged, and I felt guilty. He had men working under his command and would do as he asked. I didn't.

He closed his eyes, and his mouth moved without sound. When he stopped, he paled and collapsed to his feet. "He is coming."

That was *just* great. Léon had weakened *again*. Sebastian needed our help, and I wasn't feeling my best either. This was not a great first date.

Sebastian complained as if I was hurting him, and the two of us fell. Something moved above us, and I prayed it wasn't Noryx, then relief washed over me when I saw Jean-René.

"It's okay. Let me help." He reached for Léon first.

"No. You must take Sebastian first. Please," I begged. "Take him to Ralph and tell him to go straight to the Labyrinth. They mustn't wait for us. They must just get Sebastian to safety. And ask Sawyer to phone Mel, and tell her to meet us there, so she can give him medical attention."

Jean-René glanced at Léon, who nodded his agreement. Jean-René gave one curt nod, lifting Sebastian from the ground like he weighed nothing, and then they were gone.

I crawled to Léon, placed my body beneath his and allowed him to rest on me.

After a few minutes, Jean-René floated down, like a feather, upon return. "Okay, who's next?"

"Take Léon." I up righted him, so his friend could carry him.

"No. Take Blaire first," Léon mumbled.

"Take him, Jean-René. He can barely speak coherently." I motioned for Jean-René to do as I said.

He scooped his friend in his arms, like old lovers, and then they were gone.

I slowly rose and leaned my body against a tree trunk. Leaves rustled behind me, and I flinched.

"That was quick, Jean-René. You guys just left." I meandered around the tree and came face to face with a grinning Noryx, Shannon's little puppy.

"Where're you going, little lady?" He flicked his brown ponytail over his broad shoulder and sauntered toward me, his fiery brown eyes hinting at the pain he wanted to inflict on my body.

I backpedaled until I collided with another tree.

He grinned, flashing fangs. "I'll enjoy hurting you for Shannon." He moved so quickly he was suddenly in front of me, gripping my arms. "Shannon wants you now." He leaned forward, sniffing the nape of my neck. "You really smell delicious. I thought it was all rumors. Maybe I can have one little taste?" He made strange noises that was a mixture between a purr and an engine running. His mouth was so close to my skin and his breath against my neck that the hairs stood on end.

And I froze. Again. Like my mind couldn't figure out a way to escape this mess. I felt like a victim, and I didn't like it. Not one bit. But it wore me out. After that little explosion of mine inside the mountain, Léon's bite, and our strenuous run through the mountain, I wasn't up for more excitement. And didn't think I could survive another blood loss. I was utterly exhausted. Sebastian and Léon were safe. I could just stand here and die. Perhaps that was my destiny, at the hands of the vampire Shannon least expected it from. That made me smile. How ironic.

This could very well be my last breath. I exhaled in defeat and closed my eyes. I braced myself for Noryx's swift end of my life. Then Noryx's grip loosened around my arms. My eyes fluttered open to see a vampire who was usually calm and collected stand before me with a mask of death as he pulled a fellow vampire to shreds.

Jean-René bit Noryx's neck and pulled it until he severed his head from his body. Blood squirted everywhere and pooled at the vampire's feet. Then, with speed I'd never seen before, he removed his dead, black heart from his chest.

Noryx's body burst into flames—the front of my body was instantly hot from the heat—then it extinguished just as quickly, and ashes were all that remained. And the sudden chill in the air.

"We need to leave now, Blaire."

All I could manage was a nod before collapsing to the wet ground.

Jean-René slowly pulled me to my feet and into his arms, and then we were ascending into the night air.

Chapter Twenty-Four

I wanted to help Sebastian, but I was too weak at the moment to even stand. My healing abilities had taken a slight knock from the events of the day. Besides, Mel had shooed me away after inserting an IV line into my hand and told me to rest. While she was tending to Sebastian, Léon had his fangs in one of the blood banks—aka, a busty brunette who lived at the Labyrinth and her only job was to feed a vampire every day. And Jean-René leered at me from a chair. Somehow, he silently blamed me for everything that had happened. And to think he was the only vampire I had liked of Léon's kiss. I wanted to sic one of the werewolves on him but knew better.

I lay on a couch with that pesky drip in my hand, trying my best to ignore Jean-René, but it was difficult when I could feel tiny pinpricks crawling all over my body.

Ralph and Devan sat on the other chairs nearby, discussing with Sawyer and Marc the types of weapons we needed in case Shannon returned.

"You guys do realize that no weapon can defeat him or

any of his soldier boys," I interjected without looking at any of them.

"What would you suggest then?" Jean-René's words were clipped and dripping with malice. He had been silent the entire time, apart from the power he splashed all over me.

"A stake through the heart." I turned to meet his gaze dead on. A flurry of hot swirls slapped me in the face. I sat upright and leered at the vampire. "You know, Jean-René, I used to like you until just now. Stop it and grow up."

He smirked at me, bowed his head, and the flurries stopped.

"What is he doing to you?" Ralph asked with concern, rising from his seated position, ready to defend my honor.

"Nothing anymore," I said, getting comfortable on the couch again and ignoring the sulking vampire.

Feeling a little lightheaded after that sudden head movement, I closed my eyes. Day was about to break, and the vampires were about to retire, and thoughts of Léon and me increased my heart rate a notch. Then thoughts about how we could gently break the news to Sebastian about what had transpired between us was like an ice-cold bath, and my heart rate normalized again.

Sebastian had no idea what I had endured with that imposter vampire, Simon, and then learning Sebastian had died—but then not. The rollercoaster ride of my emotions tilted me from one side to the next, and now that I was upright again, I was about to lose my balance completely and fall to my sudden death.

My heart swelled with love for both brothers, and, for an instant, I thought perhaps I should let them both go. I would not come between them. It wasn't worth it; I could never hurt either of them, not on purpose anyway. Whose heart were we willing to sacrifice when things didn't work out? The best would be to leave now, that way it was only my heart.

Visions of Scout floated into my thoughts next along with Mason. I prayed they had gotten out of Portland. And the only thing calming my nerves was I would see them again, here, in three months' time. When Mason would be back in my life, I didn't want to be his lover again, especially after a ten-year sabbatical. We had both changed so much in those years; we weren't the same people we had first fallen in love with.

But that's only if we survived Shannon.

Then visions of test tubes, needles, and blood filled my dream. Nausea bubbled to the surface, and I wasn't sure if it was only in my dream or if I was feeling sick lying on the couch. A masked doctor holding a syringe filled with orange goo closed the gap between us and grabbed my arm. He injected the stuff into me, and, just when I thought he was finished, he snatched another syringe; this time, the stuff inside was brown. After four injections all with different shades of yuck, the doctor scanned my abdomen. He squirted cold clear jelly onto my stomach and moved the probe. He stared at the black and white monitor, fiddled with a few buttons, then the sound of a little heartbeat racing got my attention. I saw the dark-shaped bean on the monitor. Upon hearing its heartbeat, tears streaked the side of my face.

"Blaire, wake up," Léon said as he brought me from my dream.

Oh my god. I hoped I wasn't pregnant. I cannot have that, not now.

"Are you all right? You were whimpering in your sleep."

I wiped my eyes dry and swallowed a few times. "Yeah, I'm all good. How are you feeling?"

"Fine, but I'm going to lie down for the day. Mel is done with Sebastian, but he'll need you now. Are you up to it? Do you think you can walk, or do you need me to carry you to his room?"

"No thanks. I can walk," I said defensively, standing and gripping the IV line with enough force to snap it in two. But I managed not to break it and leaned on it to keep me upright. I started walking. Slowly. "We need to tell him," I whispered for his ears only.

"I know we do but not now. Wait until his strength returns. That's the least we can do, wait."

I nodded; we could wait. It didn't mean I wasn't feeling guilty, because I was. I felt awful, like flesh-eating bacteria. My hope took a nosedive.

"Could you at least remove this thing?" I asked frustratingly, raising my hand in front of his face. "I can't sleep with this in my hand." I also didn't want Sebastian to see I was still hurt. I had to be well for both of us.

Léon took my hand in his, gently freed the needle then rubbed the wound until the sting was gone. And to make things worse, he tenderly kissed my hand—the evil master vampire and his loving touches. "Ready?" he asked with a wicked grin and a wink.

"Uh-huh." I nodded, slipping the same arm through his and using him as a walking aid toward Sebastian's room.

Léon pushed open Sebastian's door. The noise must've started Sebastian, because he jackknifed from bed, making me flinch at his sudden movement. Léon was the ever-present rock for everyone to lean on. Sebastian's eyes were wide as he stared at us, through us, still trying to see us. I wasn't sure, but it was unnerving to witness. I suspected he may suffer from trauma or shock after everything that had happened to him.

"It's just us, Sebastian. You're safe," I said in a calm, soothing voice. In the dim light, I could see dirt still on one side of Sebastian's face. I unhooked myself from my walking aid and shuffled farther into the room.

Sebastian followed my every movement.

I entered the bathroom and opened the taps until the water was a pleasant temperature and left it to fill the bath.

"You're safe, brother," I heard Léon say. "I need to lie for the day. You must rest, and I'll see you later."

Upon entering the bedroom again, I saw a slight movement of Sebastian's head to let his brother know he had heard him.

Léon acknowledged me with concerned eyes then left the room.

"Come with me," I said, extending my hand for Sebastian. "A hot bath awaits your tired body."

It hurt me to watch him sit up and slowly swing his legs off the bed. I helped him stand, like the smallest movement caused him physical pain. He even walked with a slight hunched back, as if being locked in the cage had caused his spine to grow skew.

"I showered before I came to bed, you know." He smirked. Even that movement looked like it stung.

"But you didn't have my touch," I purred, wiping the dirt from his face with my free hand.

Once we were in the bathroom, I lifted his damp t-shirt; he had to bend slightly, so I could remove it completely. After pulling down his boxers, he stepped out of them, and I helped him into the bath.

He hissed at the temperature.

"It's not that hot. I'm sure your muscles need the heat."

"I'm a were-leopard, Blaire. I don't need the additional heat," he added with a wink.

"Shush and relax."

He sunk under the water to wet everything. When he came back up, I grabbed the shampoo and poured some into my hands, so I could wash his hair.

I massaged his scalp as I washed thoroughly. My movements were slow and sensual, and I poured nothing but love into each of my touches. My heart ached to see him hurt so badly, but it also jumped for joy that he was alive and back in my life. It was a very selfish thought, but I loved him, yet I shared my heart with his brother now.

My hand moved down his neck as I delicately rubbed the muscles and watched his skin pebble. When I finished, he went under the water again to rinse the shampoo.

His movements were slow and painful. Once his hair was clean, he leaned back against the edge of the bath, his shoulders sagging.

I undressed and climbed in behind him. I too needed a desperate wash. I took the loofa, added some French body wash onto it and rubbed it together, making enough foam. Once I was happy, I started on his arms, washing them and massaging gently as I went along. I didn't want to hurt him.

He closed his eyes, his mouth parting slightly, as he relaxed his head against my chest.

I continued to wash his chest, my fingers caressing some bruises that had already turned purple, while others were a pale yellow and green. I shook my head at the thought and blinked back tears. Shannon had hurt him so much during those two weeks.

My hand went over the ripples of his ribs, the bones visible under his skin. As gently as possible, I pushed his shoulders from me, so I could wash his back. Bars from the special cage he had been locked in had marked him, leaving his skin similar to that of a burn victim. He hadn't been able to shift into his black leopard to heal himself, nor had he been allowed out the cage—a cage so deadly to him, like kryptonite to Superman. Rinsing the soap off his back until all the soap was gone, I planted delicate kisses on each injured shoulder blade and was careful not to press too hard.

As gently as possible, I pulled him backward to rest against my soft chest. Luckily, I came with built-in pillows. I smiled, but I also knew pity was stamped all over my face and was grateful he couldn't see it. All I wanted to do was take it all away. I was also grateful he couldn't sense my remorse.

"You can wash the rest," I whispered and felt my cheeks flame.

He chuckled, taking the loofa from my hand, and washed the rest of his body.

I grabbed a clean loofa and washed myself.

When he was done, he leaned against me again with a long satisfactory exhale.

I wrapped my arms around his chest and left soft kisses on the side of his face. "You okay?"

"I will be now that I'm home."

Watching him relax in the bath was therapeutic. Our breathing matched up, and that was calming. A sense of belonging here with him was overwhelming, and it reminded me of the faerie who had given me a dose of my future ten years ago, and I was glad I had lost my memory six months ago. If that hadn't happened, I wouldn't be here with the men I loved.

"That's enough. The water is cold," I said.

He leaned forward to give me space to stand up and climb out the bath.

I grabbed one of the larger towels from the shelf then pulled the drain plug. I offered my hand to help him out the bath then dried his back, chest, and arms and wrapped the towel around his waist. I grabbed a fresh towel and quickly dried myself.

He grabbed fresh clothing, finished drying then dressed himself, while I did the same.

Once he was back in bed, I approached the side of the bed I always slept on and climbed in behind him. "Is this okay?" I asked as I placed my hand over his body.

He nodded slightly.

I pressed my cheek against his back and pulled him closer to my body. I curled my hand into his thin frame and flinched when I felt his ribs. They had starved him these two weeks. I wondered what else they had done.

"Do you want to talk about what Shannon did?" I whispered into his back.

"No." That one word was laced with bitterness and hate.

I kissed his back and blinked back tears. "I'm sorry."

"Why? You didn't do this to me."

Hmm, not yet, but you'll hate me soon enough, I thought, pushing the words into a dark corner. "I'm sorry all the same. For what he did, for not finding you sooner, and for not being there for you."

"It's fine. You thought I was dead. My mark was severed. I couldn't even feel my father or brother as it also destroyed those links."

"Do you want me to help you?"

"Like you helped Lance?"

"Uh-huh." I nodded into his back then left butterfly kisses across his shoulder blades.

He seemed more tired now than when I had first entered his bedroom. The bath must've taken most of his energy and didn't think he would want me to do anything else. I was just grateful he allowed me to continue holding him.

"Okay."

Just as I was about to admit defeat, he surprised me by agreeing. "What? Really?"

"Yeah, what more can happen to me?" he said, grunting in self-loathing.

It was so unlike him to be this way, but so much had happened. I needed to be patient and to be there when he needed me. Like now. I only hoped I could help him and bring *him* back to us.

"Okay, we can continue to lie like this. I'm just going to concentrate on you. It shouldn't hurt. But if it does, let me know, and I'll stop."

He mumbled *hmm*, and I closed my eyes to give him my full attention. I lowered my metal shield that surrounded my aura and treasure chest full of tricks, and it slowly slipped through my hand and into him. My aura hovered near his heart first; it was strong and good. But that speck of evil was still there. It was that same spec I had seen after I helped Moonrise when she drank that poisonous tea and I had tried to help Sebastian. But I knew that evil wasn't Sebastian but his connection with the were-leopards, the connection to that man who had killed Ma. I wanted to know more, so I concentrated on that spec.

"Rick?" Sebastian blurted, slightly exasperated.

"What?"

"I don't know what you're doing, but you're conjuring Rick, Anne's husband. He used to be the leap's alpha."

Shit. Please don't tell me that was who had hurt Ma, and I had killed in revenge. I'd never known the man's true name. All I knew about him was what he looked and sounded like. If it really was him, I couldn't let Sebastian, Anne, or her children know it had been me who had killed Rick. It would break them and tear Sebastian and me apart. And I wasn't sure what would hurt Sebastian more—that I had killed his surrogate father or that I was in love with his brother.

Today was not my day.

"What is it, Blaire?" Sebastian asked, half panicked.

I had to keep him calm or help him try to forget what I had just dug up.

"*Shh*, let me finish," I blurted and pushed more of my aura into him to settle him down; fortunately, my party box was full of neat tricks.

He went quiet beneath my touch and relaxed.

My aura moved from his heart in search of *him*, his true self—that flame that kept Sebastian alive, that same flame that sets him apart from everyone else, his life essence that was unique and what I was totally in love with. When I found my aura swarming in darkness, I knew it was Shannon who had done that to him. In those two weeks, Shannon had beaten him to a pulp, metaphysically, and had drained him of his life, physically, and had left his soul in the dark depths of despair.

But I had found his flame. It was tucked in the depths of something so evil it could only have been Shannon. With my white aura, I scooped his flame in the palm of my hands and placed it where it belonged, wrapping it in a cage where no one could touch or move it again.

Sebastian sucked in air, and I felt his chest move as his lungs expanded. Those ribs I could feel beneath my touch had filled out with the muscle he had always had. His breathing steadied, and a low guttural sound emanated from within him, followed by a husky growl which echoed off the walls.

It sent all the hairs on my body to stand on end.

His flame flared to life, bright and captivating, like it was always meant to be.

I brought my aura up my arm and locked it tightly behind my steel walls and opened my eyes.

Chapter Twenty-Five

Sebastian stared at me with his eyes and mouth wide open. "Is that what it feels like when you bring people back from their untimely death?"

"Something like that." My grin stretched from ear to ear. "How do you feel now?"

"Better than ever," he said, sitting up, like he was just injected with a shot of adrenaline. He looked like he always did—the Sebastian I had lost two weeks ago, the man I loved. He was no longer the emaciated were-leopard with one foot in the grave.

I was sure I looked goofy with my wide grin, but I was ecstatic to know I could help him. I jumped on top of him and planted kisses all over his face.

He chuckled at my display of affection; that was the best sound of the day—his healthy laugh.

It brought warmth to my heart, and I wanted to burst with glee. I had that schoolgirl crush all over again. "Hearing your laugh made everything worth it. I was so worried I'd never see *you* again." I climbed off him, so I could concentrate on him and not his body.

His eyes glistened like emeralds. He was keeping his emotions in check, tucking them behind his own steel barrier. "I'm touched you felt that way, but you shouldn't have put yourself in harm's way for me."

That wasn't the response I was hoping for, and my heart dropped to the pit of my stomach. I sat back and frowned at him. Now that he had some energy, he was using it to complain about his rescue.

"If I had known you were still alive, I would've come to find you sooner. And I don't care about getting hurt. I would've asked everyone to help me get you out of there as soon as we knew where you were. It was by chance we were there, and Shannon's vampire had found us first." My voice was raised, and I sounded angry, even to myself. "And another thing, it's not negotiable that we were out looking for you. Besides, you would've done the same for me or anyone else you care for."

He playfully smacked the side of my thigh and ass. "Naughty, Blaire, but you're right. I would've rallied the masses to find you or anyone I cared for." He yawned. "It's just Shannon isn't someone who we should handle with kid gloves, and you could've gotten hurt." He gently brushed hair out of my face, a tenderness in his eyes. "We need to devise a strategy to get rid of him quickly and cleanly." His face was all business-like, serious and full of revenge. He ended his little speech with another yawn, and I knew it was enough talking for now. He was exhausted, and here we were talking about it. He needed to rest, and so did I. We could plan our revenge after we had slept a few hours.

"You're right. We need to do all those things, but now we need to sleep." I slipped my arm around his waist again.

He turned, so he could bring me into the curve of his body. We were a perfect fit. "You have no idea how much I've missed holding you like this," he said into the nape of my neck, sending goosebumps all over my body. "I missed all of you. It's all I thought about while ..." I heard him swallow whichever memory had haunted him that very second. "When I was a hostage to the darkness, it's all that kept me going. That's when I realized the mark was gone when I couldn't reach out to you. I thought when Kasdeya had broken our bond, you had died, that it was impossible for a human to survive what you went through. But, as time moved on, somehow, I felt a small spark of hope that you were okay, that you had survived, and that I would hold you again, like I am now. I don't know what I would've done if I didn't have that hope to hold on to." His voice broke with the last sentence, his emotions pushing to the surface.

I gripped his arms tighter while he pulled me in closer. I could melt into him. My emotions finally hit home, and the tears fell, dampening his pillow.

He heard my whimpering and moved so he could lift my chin toward him to look into my watery eyes, and he kissed me.

At first, I too thought Sebastian was dead; we all had, except Anne. She had said he had to be alive, because his spirit wasn't with the other spirit were-leopards. She had explained that when one of their own died, their spirit joined the leap metaphysically, and his hadn't done that. That's when I had agreed that Sebastian had to be alive. That flicker of hope had kept me going and everyone around us. If I hadn't had that hope, I wasn't sure what would've happened.

"Me too, Sebastian," I whispered.

Yep, until Léon and I tell him what had happened between us, it would definitely kill him then.

What have we done?

"*Ma chérie*, wake up," Léon whispered near my ear while caressing my face.

I opened my eyes.

"You need to come with me, but do not disturb him." He jerked his chin in Sebastian's direction.

I wiped my eyes. "What's wrong, Léon?"

"Come."

Slowly and delicately, I lifted Sebastian's arm off me and scooted from the bed.

He moved but fell asleep again.

I followed Léon outside the room and closed the door behind me. "Did something happen?" I yawned, wiping sleep from my eyes.

Salvador flew around the corner in a hurry and joined us.

Something in the way he moved and stared at me made me feel uneasy.

"Kitten." He kissed the top of my head.

A cold feeling washed over me the way Salvador had said his nickname for me mixed in with the bit of affection. I glanced from one vampire to the other and frowned. "What is it?" I folded my arms. "The way the two of you are staring at me is freaking me out."

Léon started to say something then stopped.

"If you won't tell her, I will," Salvador threatened.

"No," Léon said, frowning at his father, then stared at me warily, the way one would a skittish horse, as if I needed to be calmed down. "We received a message from Shannon."

Now that got my full attention. I just stared back at him, waiting for him to continue.

"He has Scout."

In that instance, my world crumbled. "What? How?" I muttered, stepping backward, as if I needed all the space to myself, hitting my head against the wall behind me. I scowled as I rubbed the back of my head.

"He must have had someone following you from Chicago," Léon suggested.

"Where is Shannon? What does he want?" I asked, my vision slightly blurry from the sudden surge of anger coursing through me.

"He wants you," Salvador retorted.

"Well, he can have me. I won't sit idly by when that monster has my child," I said with venom, and, just as I was about to return to the room to get dressed, the door opened.

"What are you doing out here?" Sebastian asked with his hand still on the door handle.

I wrapped my arms around his waist. The instant I felt his warm body against mine, I couldn't stop the tears from falling.

"Sebastian! You look"—Salvador waved his hands in the air — "wonderful!"

"It was all her. She worked her magic and made me whole again." He kissed the top of my head.

I glanced at Léon, whose demeanor had not changed. It was still like marble—cold, smooth, yet somehow sharp around the edges.

His gaze flitted to me then to his brother.

In that second, I saw his discomfort at my obvious affections for the other man in my life. I hated this. I didn't want to lie to anyone anymore. I pleaded with my eyes when Léon glanced at me again. I didn't want to go against Shannon with this hanging over our heads. I wanted to tell Sebastian what had happened and, if he hated me, then fine, at least we could all move forward. But I couldn't carry on like this; one of us would always feel left out and hurt.

"Father, will you excuse us?" Léon asked Salvador.

"Good luck, son." He squeezed Léon's shoulder then sauntered down the corridor. Their metaphysical connection was still intact, and Salvador must've realized what Léon wanted to say to Sebastian.

"Can we speak with you, Sebastian?" Léon asked, all the while watching me.

I nodded in understanding what he was silently asking me.

Once we were inside the room again, Léon closed the door and leaned against the wood as he stared at us.

Sebastian narrowed his eyes at his brother then at me. He stiffened knowingly as he swallowed hard enough for me to hear and pressed his lips into a straight line. He exhaled audibly. It seemed like he was accepting whatever he had just thought of, and that he knew something had happened between Léon and me. Lifting his one hand, he said, "I don't want to know about it. If the looks you two are giving me are anything to go by, perhaps it's none of my business. Don't tell me at all."

"It is your business, and I need to tell you, Sebastian," I pleaded, the back of my throat tightening as tears threatened to burst through the floodgates again with no way of stopping them.

"No, Blaire," he said, shaking his head. "I don't need to know." He paused. Staring down at me, he added, "Do you love me?"

"Yes." I nodded.

"Do you love Léon?"

I glanced at Léon then at Sebastian. "Yes," I answered sheepishly, staring at my feet.

Sebastian exhaled a shaky breath, but he didn't let go of me or push me away. He did something that took me by surprise; he squeezed my waist and kissed my temple. Then he stared at his brother for what felt like a very long time. We could've heard a pin drop it was so quiet.

My pulse thundered in my ears as we waited in anticipation. I was close to Sebastian's heart, and that too was beating harder. He wasn't happy. I was afraid he would let go of me and attack Léon.

"If I asked her to choose, one of us would come up short. Who knows what that would do to us?" He pointed at Léon then himself to emphasize his meaning. "What I know is I don't want to lose Blaire. Not now. Not ever. I know she pulls you in just as much as me, and honestly, I cannot blame you. I must commend you though, brother. You restrained yourself very well."

I didn't have to look at Sebastian to know he smiled at that.

"From the moment she came into our lives, everything has changed." He kissed the top of my head and pulled me in closer to him. "You thought I was dead, and then you didn't know if you would ever see me again. It's complicated, and it may only get worse. I don't know what the future holds for any of us. But I'm willing to share. I've never before, but I'm sure we can work ... something out." He whispered the last sentence as if it hurt to say it.

The silence was deafening after Sebastian spoke. Léon stared at him with an open mouth; I had never seen so much expression on that vampire's face before—complete and utter shock, unless it was relief that hit his face, but I couldn't help but smile either way.

I hugged Sebastian closer to me. "I thought I would lose you a second time when we told you what had happened between Léon and me. I was so afraid." I stared up at him, my eyes filled with unshed tears. Again.

Léon's usual stone expression was back on, and he pulled Sebastian and me into a group hug.

Red tears stained Sebastian's shirt.

"Right," Léon said once he broke up the embrace. "Now that that is out of the way"—he grinned, wiping the red stains off his face— "we can rescue Blaire's daughter."

Chapter Twenty-Six

Everybody wanted to help me rescue Scout and Mason. Ralph and Devan were already here waiting for the rescue party to start. Léon and Sebastian were busy gearing up with Sawyer and Marc. Even Salvador was here, with his dark-winged daemon named Verin.

Most shifters wanted to help; Anne with her two children and some were-leopards offered everyone refreshments. Arturo and his were-rats discussed weapons and which ones they had available. The Chicago were-rats were on their way and would meet with us later in the evening. Troy and some of his were-lions reviewed tactics and the various forms of attacks with Shawn and his werewolves. Those who knew how to fight stood with their muscles flexing with power.

A whirlwind of emotions couldn't stay hidden, and I had cried at the thought that Scout was kidnapped, again, yet relieved so many people had wanted to stand behind me —with me—and fight. We were like an extended family, not by blood but by shared kinship, who were banding together to retrieve one of our own.

Once I had composed myself, I finally joined everybody on the dancefloor. Yeah, we were in *Kiss*, because it was the only place that could fit most of us at once without having to go outside.

Léon and Sebastian stood side by side. As I entered, they looked up and eyed me at the same time. I approached them and put an arm around each of their waists, pulling them in closer. Standing in their embraces was like a warm comfortable blanket. I was sure we got a few stares, but I didn't care. I was content. Ralph whistled behind me then chuckled. It made me smile; at least my work partner had my back.

The discussion volleyed about what we would do and how it would be done, which guns were best to use against Shannon and his soldiers, which ammo might kill them off quicker, where everybody would meet at the rendezvous, and who would stand where.

I zoned out for most of the talk. I thought about what that man was doing to my daughter. I was going into full-on mama-bear mode; just thinking about him touching her enraged me. I was ready to fight tooth and nail. And now.

"Blaire?" Sebastian said near my ear.

I flinched, glancing at him; he was blurry around the edges. "Yeah?" I blinked in quick succession until I could see him clearer.

He rubbed his forearms. "Your anger, it's spiking a couple of volts, and your hands and feet are glowing."

"Sorry," I said but didn't mean it. I concentrated on my blinding hot rage, trying to tuck it where it belonged before I shifted into my saber in front of everyone. That would be funny, but I didn't care. I should care, but I guess my *cup runneth over*, and I was all out of fucks to give.

My arms pebbles. I glanced over my shoulder. Both Ralph and Devan were staring at me. I shrugged.

Devan came closer. "I sense a change in you. But it's more than just your memory returning."

I wasn't sure what he meant by that; I hadn't felt any changes. Unless he was referring to my saber, or me and the brothers.

"Don't look so worried." He touched my shoulder and shifted knowingly. Whatever he saw when he had touched me put him at ease, and he smiled at me.

My smile mirrored his, except his was more contagious. It was a smile reserved for adorable puppies and cute kids. I was neither.

He released my shoulder and gave a curt nod to imply that was all he would say on the subject. "Are you ready?" he asked, surveying everyone in the dance club.

"Of course, I'm ready. This is my child we're talking about. I'll do whatever it takes to get her back."

"Good." He nodded once. "'Cause we'll need your full attention."

It was strange and refreshing to hear him speak to me like that—full of confidence and pride. I suspected he knew I had missed the entire conversation about our rescue mission. My mind wasn't in the here and now; I was too busy plotting all the things I would do to Shannon when I got my little hands around his neck.

After my impromptu discussion with Devan, I tried to follow what they had agreed upon for us to rescue Scout. Shannon had said I had to come on my own. He would know if I wasn't, and he would hurt Scout in a way that would cause any parent to see red. I already saw red, and I wanted to spill it from his lifeless body.

Léon had already notified the Vampire Council of Shannon's wrongdoings, and they had tasked Alex and Morticia to pass down judgement. I suspected they didn't ask Genevieve to assist, considering I didn't like her rotting talents the last time we had met. They would arrive shortly.

We agreed the humans couldn't know what was about to happen. It was only recently that humans were comfortable with the various monsters living among them. And they had just settled on the fact a vampire wanted to run for governor. It would cause chaos if the humans discovered what Shannon had done or was about to do; and a war between the monsters and the humans would only end in carnage. None of the monsters wanted that; we only wanted Shannon and his soldiers gone.

We couldn't include the small police force either, as they wouldn't know how to handle any situation where monsters were involved. So it was just us assassins and the monsters who would handle it in silence. Shannon's death had to be seen as an accident and not something by the Vampire Council. It was a tricky situation.

The shifters agreed on something; I still wasn't sure what that was though. When everyone started leaving the nightclub, I turned to Léon and Sebastian and asked what the next steps were.

"Weren't you paying attention?" Sebastian teased.

"No, sorry. My mind was elsewhere."

As if sensing my unease, he didn't continue teasing but informed me about what we would do. I would meet Shannon at the agreed place and at the agreed time. But everyone who could fight would surround me. Everyone would keep their distance, because no one wanted Scout to get hurt if Shannon sensed others near. That gave us six hours before I had to meet him. I still had time to mentally prepare myself for the meeting. And if I wanted to be ready, I needed to get out of my head, get out of the *Mommy mind* and into my *assassin mind.*

I nodded my agreement and approached the exit that would lead us inside the Labyrinth. Léon and Sebastian followed close behind me, and I think Ralph said something about joining us too. I wasn't paying him any attention either. My mind was reeling with possibilities of failure and of success and what each of those would mean. But one thing was clear; I wouldn't make it if they hurt Scout. Now that I had my memories back, if I lost Scout, I would unravel completely.

As I reached the door that led into the Labyrinth, an explosion rocked the nightclub. I braced myself by reaching for the door handle with my feet firmly apart. The middle section of the roof collapsed, and the ceiling rained onto the shifters still in the middle of the dancefloor. Glass exploded into the club, cutting into everyone like shrapnel, tearing pieces of my clothing and spilling my blood.

Léon and Sebastian hovered protectively over me, but, by then, it was too late. I was already hurt.

But I didn't feel it. I was too numb.

Before me was carnage though. Bodies lay on the floor beneath cement blocks, while parts of the fallen ceiling and roof trapped others. Some were-animals shifted into their beasts to heal, but some wouldn't see the light of day ever again.

Flecks of power beat against my body, and I wondered for a split second who was putting on the display. The heat from the flare up was like fuel to my already fragile mind. Then I heard laughter somewhere above us. I glanced up and saw Soldier Boy with a smile stretched across his face as he floated through the hole in the ceiling toward us. I wanted to permanently wipe that smug look off his face.

And, as Soldier Boy floated down, five more Soldier Boys joined him. They stayed hovering just above us.

Those still alive watched in awe as these monster soldiers paraded in front of us like they were about to be crowned. Those who had shifted into their beasts growled, readying themselves for attack. The first one jumped and bit one soldier. They fought when they crashed to the ground; another wolf joined his brother as they fought the soldier together. That's when more Soldier Boys entered the nightclub and attacked the closest were-animal to them. A were-rat had locked teeth around the arm of one. A were-leopard was going head to head with another. Cries, growls, and howls were followed by blood—lots of blood where they fell. And I couldn't allow more of these were-animals to die. One after the other, more beasts fell to their deaths.

Unfortunately, when one Soldier Boy was killed, another flew inside the nightclub to take his brother's place. It was as if Shannon had made an endless supply of Soldier Boys for him to play with as he pleased.

Sebastian and Léon were getting ready to fight when Salvador stepped forward with his daemon, and he did what he did well; he clapped. The power emanating from his fingertips hit everyone like an exploding mushroom cloud. It blew everyone back a few spaces. But, instead of shredding the Soldier Boys like his power did to vampires, it did nothing—absolutely fucking nothing. It only stopped everyone from fighting to see who had put on such a massive display of power.

We needed to do something else if we were to stop them.

Salvation

That first Soldier Boy hovered where he was and stared at me the entire time.

Bunching my hands into fists, I wanted to hurt him. Lowering my shields, my aura burst through instantly. My white anger was hot like coals. My feet and hands glowed. "Get back, boys," I growled before my anger exploded around everyone. A second after they had moved, I screamed my frustration, my hurt, and my rage. My clothing tore off my body and rained like confetti.

Ralph and Devan gasped like two schoolgirls and cowered behind the bar.

Léon and Sebastian stood closer to me, to my big furry saber body.

Soldier Boy's smirk was now gone, and his eyes were round like saucers.

Without thinking, I reflexively leaned back on my hind legs and pounced as hard as I could onto Soldier Boy. I opened my large jaw and went directly for his throat.

It was just pure luck and him being dumbstruck by my little demonstration that he didn't react in time. He was made with all sorts of monster DNA and molded into this perfect killing machine for Shannon. Yet, I had shocked him for a second, which gave me enough time to attack. I wondered whether the rest could learn from one of their mistakes. I hoped not, but then again, I doubted I could do that ever again.

I gripped his body between my claws and locked my jaw. I bit his throat, blood pouring into my mouth, and I drank him down. His blood was flavored with some spice I couldn't quite place, but it wasn't unpleasant nor was it natural—synthetic. I snapped Soldier Boy's neck and ripped his head from his body. Cushioning my fall with Soldier Boy's limp corpse, we crashed to the ground with a loud thump. The other Soldier Boys stared unknowingly at me; the were-animals still alive stood back and gawked.

I felt like a freak but didn't care; I just wanted my daughter back. And I could only do that by going through one Soldier Boy at a time.

Before I could pounce and kill the other Solider Boys, a slow clap echoed inside the nightclub.

Chapter Twenty-Seven

All eyes followed the dark figure who was clapping. His blond hair swept his shoulders as he floated near the hole in the building's ceiling—an easy exit should he need it. Six more Soldier Boys hovered around him, his personal guards.

Through my animal's eyes, I had a better view of them. They weren't clones of one, but like the others, they all had striking similarities—their dark piercing blank gaze, chiseled facial features, and flexed energy-filled muscles. The only differences were their hair color. Were they there for Shannon's protection from us or just from me? My lip curled and hooked on a large tooth. A grunting noise escaped my mouth.

Movement near the bar caught my attention. Ralph and Devan stood against the wall and closer to the door that led into the Labyrinth. I could only assume it was so they could escape the madness about to happen.

Sebastian moved next, and an explosion of his own clothes rained on everyone as he changed into his large black beast. His transition was magnificent, like liquid mercury. There were no sounds of the usual bones breaking, tendons snapping, and reknitting. It was quick, efficient, and it seemed relatively pain free. A long sawing roar echoed within the club as he moved to stand closer to me.

I scent marked him, my head rubbing under his chin, then he mine.

Shannon seemed half shocked that Sebastian had healed so quickly and could shift into his beast so easily.

I smirked at the thought but not for long; it was game time.

Léon and Salvador did their own levitating, hovering, vampire thing until they were face to face with Shannon.

"You're surrounded, Shannon," Salvador said with an air of authority that made me shiver. "Give up the girl and her father before things"—he shrugged as if it meant everything and nothing — "get out of hand."

"I know what you can do, Salvador, but in case you didn't notice, your clap did nothing to my soldiers," Shannon said staring at Salvador for a moment too long.

They shared a history I wasn't aware of. And I wondered if it had anything to do with why Salvador couldn't tell me his real name when I was younger. He had said it was for my safety. It would all make sense; Salvador knew things about me and wanted to keep me safe. He was my protector. And, since vampires could smell lies and if I had said I didn't know Salvador back then, it was the truth. My heart burst with love for the old vampire, and I was lucky to have him in my life.

Salvador shifted uncomfortably at Shannon's cold words. He knew his clap did not affect the Soldier Boys as he had hoped. We needed another plan and fast. But then I heard Shannon continue with his words and a growl trickled from between my large teeth.

"I only want what is rightfully mine," Shannon said, turning his fiery gaze to me with what I could only describe as a cheerful face, which didn't make any sense.

"I'm not yours to keep, Shannon."

"You are mistaken, little one." Shannon floated to the ground.

His Soldier Boys followed him, with Léon and Salvador hot on their heels.

Shannon touched the ground and approached me. When his left hand touched my head, I was hit with certain memories—flashes of test tubes, large and small needles, beds, monitors, an incubator, and the last one was of my mother, a much younger version of her when she could still see. Her eyes were crystal blue, her smile pure, and she was rubbing her swollen belly. My father was there too, standing against the far door, dressed in a uniform with a gun over his shoulder.

The visions caused me physical pain, like a carving knife slicing pieces of skin off my back. I shuddered at the icy sensation, which pushed my saber into her cave. My leopard, rat, lion, and wolf watched me from the safety of their caves; they looked as scared as I felt.

I awoke on my hands and knees in my human form in my birthday suit. Tears streaked my face, wetting the debris beneath me. When I raised my head, Léon was busy putting his jacket over me. I rose, fastening the jacket closed and muttering a *thank you* in appreciation.

"What was that, Shannon?" I asked hoarsely. The back of my throat felt like I had swallowed shards of glass from the floor.

"I made you who you have become."

The silence cut through the nightclub, like the reaper with his scythe.

Sebastian nuzzled my cold hand, but I couldn't move.

I blinked at Shannon. "What does that mean?"

"Exactly what I just said. But I see you're in shock, so I'll explain it to you. Your mother was desperate for a child and needed medical treatment. I needed a test subject for my experiments, so we made a deal." His smile stretched across his pale face, and, for a split second, I thought I saw horns popping from his forehead. Shannon licked his lips. "For years I had been experimenting, first on animals then on a human or two. Then your mother came into my life. She was part fae, part witch, and her uterus was just right for what I wanted to do. You were healthy and grew till full term without complications. But, after she delivered you, she ran off with one of my guards. Our deal was the first baby would be mine, and the second one she could keep. But she disappeared before the exchange could take place. She masked her scent very well, and I couldn't trace her or that useless guard who was supposed to bring her back to me." Shannon paced. "I thought I had lost you forever until I met you at the dinner." He stopped and stared at me.

Léon shifted uncomfortably beside me, and I shrunk into myself, but, no matter how small I felt, he was there for the picking.

"But I knew Léon and Sebastian would keep you safe. Then I realized it was your daughter I had been after all those years ago." His grin returned, and his eyes flashed darker. "Noryx and two others followed you to Portland and saw your family fleeing, like the boogeyman was chasing them, and he went after them. He brought them back here for me, and wow, Scout is definitely a prize worth fighting for."

Salvation

Again, my body acted without informing my brain what was happening, and I lunged at Shannon. I latched my legs around his waist and dug my fingernails into his face until I drew blood. I dragged my fingernails down his cheeks, scraping chunks of flesh along the way.

Shannon screamed and tried to pull my arms from his face while three Soldier Boys tried to pull me off him.

I was in attack mode, and all I saw was red.

The Soldier Boys pried me off Shannon, but the damage I had caused was done; it wasn't enough.

He burst out laughing as his skin knitted together again. "Release her, boys."

The two who held my arms let go while the third one slowly released his arm from my neck. As he pulled, I gripped his arm and bit it. He shrilled in pain as I ripped a chunk from his forearm. Soldier Boy on my right elbowed me in the face.

My nose stung, and my eyes watered, and I released his buddy. "Don't touch me again." I spit out the piece of flesh. "I guess you created an animal, Shannon." I leered sinisterly at him, leaving the blood to drip down my chin.

He chuckled and nodded. "Yes, it would seem that way, but you're still mine."

Shit, I guess my chewing on one of his boys didn't deter him from me.

Shannon levitated again. "Bring her, boys."

Soldier Boys gripped me, painfully this time to ensure I didn't hurt any of them again, and we floated up.

"If you stop us, Salvador, Léon, or Sebastian, I will not hesitate to kill the girl," Shannon said when he saw Léon approach him.

I felt everyone stiffen as one. No one budged from their spot.

Léon's eyes pleaded with me. He wanted to hurt Shannon. And I couldn't blame him, so did I, but I couldn't afford anything to happen to Scout.

We didn't know where she was or who was tasked with watching her. We didn't know anything at this point. I wanted them to take me, then I could see where they were and possibly try to escape. Or die trying. But Scout had to be rescued first.

I shook my head. "No, Léon, you need to stay. I need to find Scout." I winked at him, ensuring none of the soldiers could see.

Chapter Twenty-Eight

During my flight with the three Soldier Boys, one had slipped a black-material bag over my head, so I couldn't see where we were going. But that didn't matter; the GPS in my earrings didn't need to see where I was going to know where I would end up. I had slipped in the earrings when I had arrived at the Labyrinth from Portland. And I was sure Léon and Sebastian would know how to find me. They were resourceful creatures. Well, that was my experience with the brothers so far.

During the *flight*, my mind was wrapped around what Shannon had revealed, that I was a test-tube baby, an experiment, something he had conjured up with whatever he had used on my mother to create me. I was not *natural* in any sense of the word. It explained so much. And that my dad—the man I had grown up to love as my dad—wasn't really my birth father. He was just a guard tasked with keeping my mother from running away. They must've fallen in love during her pregnancy and planned her escape soon after the birth.

Everything made sense.

The reason why I was homeschooled was to ensure no opportunities occurred for anyone to kidnap me or ask pressing questions about who I was, why Ma had always told me never to reveal my true self, that I should *never* trust anyone with our family history, of who my mom and *dad* were. And it explained why no pictures of them existed.

I felt ill. Nausea built within the pit of my stomach. It could've been a combination of the flying, the quick change into my saber and then into my human form again, and these shocking revelations that were making my head and stomach spin. I still wanted to gouge out Shannon's eyes though.

When we finally touched ground, and with the material bag still over my head, I saw my bare feet. We walked on wet sand then a sidewalk. We walked for a few minutes until we reached a step, and then white floors were beneath my feet and the clicking of everyone's steel-tip boots against the tiles. When we stopped, they removed the bag from my head. Blinding lights singed my eyes. I had to immediately stare at the flawless and shiny white tiles under my dirty feet and cover my eyes until I had adjusted to the room's brightness. The air smelled clean with a hint of lemon and sterilizer.

My heart raced in my ribcage. An overwhelming sense of familiarity and dread coursed through my veins.

"Look at me, Blaire," Shannon commanded.

Slowly lifting my head, I removed my hands from my eyes. I took in the room—clean, very painfully clean white walls, polished silver shelves, silver gurneys, silver and white equipment, and a white ceiling. A stark contrast to the labs in the mountain.

Shannon smiled, and it was quite endearing. "You're magnificent, Blaire. And to think you're my first child."

Did I hear him right? That I was *his* child? "Excuse me?"

"Wow, it felt good to finally say that out loud. You. Are. My. Child."

I flinched when he placed a hand on each of my shoulders.

"Relax, Blaire. I won't hurt you. I could never hurt you." Tenderness gleamed in his sparkly blue eyes.

"Then what do you want with me and my daughter?"

"Only a few drops of your blood, that is all."

I was still confused, and it must've shown on my face.

"Sit." Shannon pushed me toward a steel chair. "Now that we're alone, I can share your real-life story with you." He sat on the chair opposite me. "As I said earlier, your mom wanted a child, and I needed a test subject to carry my child. Even though I am nearly as old as Salvador and knew of him having his own sons, I wanted the same and tested my sperm. I only had a few viable options for use. I wasn't sure they would still work as they should, but your mom's ovaries were pristine. And with the regular injections I gave her concocted with particular hormones, my sperm with her egg, everything worked out perfectly. The result was *you*."

I snorted in disbelief. "You're my *real* dad?"

He nodded, cupping one side of my face with his large palm. "Yes, you are *my* child, *my* flesh and *my* blood."

"Are there others?" I swallowed hard. "Like me?"

He shook his head, and his expression softened. "No. After you, they kept dying. I was running out of viable sperm and couldn't replicate the original process I had with your mother. Unfortunately, I had to perform abortions on the mothers who, we later discovered, could not have any more children. Some subjects died during the procedures, with a handful dying at their own hands."

I realized he regarded them as mere subjects and not humans with families, feelings, and lives. Anger boiled within me. "Why did you bother continuing when you knew what you were doing wasn't working? You were killing innocent women and their unborn children."

"They were nothing but specs on a screen. They never reached any real gestational age. They all withered and seized to exist within the first trimester. And, if you were with me, I wouldn't have needed to do any of it." His anger rose as he spoke louder. His voice echoed off the walls and what felt like pins raining on me.

Now I knew where I got my temper from. Ma was always the calm soul, Shannon not so much.

"But your mother disappeared with you before I could draw any of your blood or run any tests. I couldn't even pick up your scent. No trace of you existed at all. I suspected she cloaked you, so I could never find you. That is why I needed to continue. I couldn't stand idly by and wait. I had to make another one of *you*. That was until I met the Haiti twins and their lovely girlfriend."

I gasped. "It was you?" It all made sense now, all the events that had happened, that had led us to this very moment. My attack, the twins, the poison that was killing the were-animals were for him to control them and for me to finally meet my maker—*Dad*. I groaned inwardly. I would rather die than call him anything relating to that.

"I found the twins first, and their blood was a great addition to my collection. But before I could finish and let them go, she came to get them. You must understand I always let the specials go. Always. But their girlfriend rescued them before I could finalize my tests, which angered me. I had them followed, and, when she was alone, I took her, experimented on her. Then I thought, because she was a *special* who could travel from one body to the next, that she would be a viable candidate for IVF. But again, it was unsuccessful, and she kept bleeding after the evacuation of the fetus."

Blood drained from my body. He was truly the monster of all monsters, playing Frankenstein in the modern ages. "Why did you remove her tongue and her ears?" A distinct bad taste of bile filled my mouth.

"She wouldn't shut up!" he snarled.

"And you thought it was okay to torture her?"

"I didn't torture her ... that much." He shrugged.

"You removed her ears and her tongue, then you damaged the body she was in, so she could never have children. Then they came after me." I shook my head, trying not to relive the memory, and swallowed hard again. "All you did was damage people, Shannon. Damage families. You're the true monster everyone should be afraid of." My words were soft and slow, dripping with malice.

Shannon grew angrier. He towered over me and was monstrous. Something that resembled a horn on either side of his forehead protruded through his skin. It was like his anger made him bigger, turning him into some other creature with horns I had never seen before.

I wondered if he dabbled in his own medicine and had created this monster that lived deep within him that reared its ugly head when he was angry, similar to what my anger made me change into—my saber. Except, he reminded me of the Devil. I stepped backward. If he shifted into his beast for real, I wouldn't want to be in the firing line of *that* explosion.

"I only wanted to help us monsters to be the best we could, to become what we were always meant to be." His voice deepened, like rolling thunder. "To rule humans and make them our slaves."

"Rubbish. Us mystical people are already powerful enough. We just had to tap into our available resources and use it to our advantage. The humans already fear us. We're already gods in their eyes." My voice was low, dark, and imposing. I was trying to be as scary as him but wasn't sure I was pulling it off, because he chuckled, albeit nervously.

"You're so naïve, Blaire." His voice sounded like his usual baritone. He was calming down. As quickly as he had grown, he shrank to his usual height. "Yet you're so lovable and pure. My sweet, Blaire."

"I am not *your* Blaire. Never have, never will be."

"When Sebastian was at his weakest, I had to have him." Shannon added while pacing.

Which meant I had made Sebastian weak because of our relationship, or was it because of our link that we shared?

"It was unfortunate what Simon did to you though. If it means anything, he took you without my knowledge. I requested both Sebastian *and* you, but Simon went against my orders. Thank you for punishing him for me." Shannon smiled darkly. "Because Sebastian is both a vampire and a were-animal, I suspected he held some sort of missing DNA link to ensure my embryos could grow. And you know what? They grew, and quickly. I had to adjust the genetic markers, but that was quick, and I could finally produce my soldiers." He glanced proudly at his men who surrounded us.

I couldn't keep it down; I spewed projectile vomit everywhere. I was too late to block it from landing all over the floor.

The two soldiers tending to me groaned as they averted their eyes to the vomit, while one of them brought a wet cloth for my mouth. Another one mopped and turned pale; I think it was their first time cleaning up vomit.

I celebrated a small win without showing them my satisfaction.

Another handed me white clothing, since I was still naked under Léon's now soiled coat.

"Are you all right?" Shannon asked, sounding like a slice of concern was somewhere in those words, but I didn't want any of his sympathy.

I ignored him.

"Thank you, boys. Blaire, dress quickly then come. Your daughter awaits you." He headed toward the door.

Chapter Twenty-Nine

Once I was dress in what seemed to be hospital garments, I followed silently behind Shannon through a long hallway. The clicking of his dress shoes against the tiles was like glass slicing down my back. Each step was a cut, like nails on a chalkboard, a blade between nail and skin, digging in. One false move and it could pierce the skin, drawing blood. I shuddered and walked slower. But a Soldier Boy behind me pushed me forward every time I slowed.

Once inside a room, Shannon entered a combination into a large vault—a panic room—to reveal Mason and Scout lying on their own beds, waking from a nap.

Scout's eyes widened when she saw me. She jumped off her bed and darted toward me.

I braced for impact as she hit my body like a truck and wrapped her skinny arms around me. "Are you okay?" I asked, kissing her forehead.

"Uh-huh," she said and continued holding on.

"Did he hurt you?"

"No. They've just locked us up in here the whole time until now."

"Mason can stay, but you two need to come with me."

My eyes silently apologized to Mason as Shannon edged us out the vault while one of his soldiers snapped it shut with a loud whoosh of air and locked it.

Shannon motioned us to the two gurneys where trays of needles lay waiting for us. "I only want some blood, that is all. I'm not here to hurt either of you, but if you don't do as I want, you leave me no choice." He raised an eyebrow in exclamation.

"I'll go first," I said, rolling up a sleeve.

Shannon did as he said and only took one vial of blood from each of us. He instructed us to stay where we were while he ran some tests at a station in the next room.

Two Soldier Boys watched our every move. I had a sinking feeling Shannon had instructed them to use deadly force if I tried anything. Both soldiers kept their hands on the large black weapons strapped across their fronts.

I couldn't risk doing anything just yet. I needed to unarm the soldiers, open the vault to free Mason and then get out. I couldn't do it all on my own. Another problem was I didn't know how many Soldier Boys Shannon had made. Therefore, I could either wait for the cavalry or first see what my chances were here. Right now, I needed to hold Scout in my arms. It would be a comfort to me, a mother holding her child.

I lay with Scout on one gurney, holding onto her for dear life.

She explained what had happened, that the vampire Noryx had said I was in an accident, and they should go with him. Bad move, *stranger danger*, but they didn't know who he was or what was happening. They willingly went with him, and he had brought them here, locking them in the vault until just now.

I was just glad to have her with me again. Unharmed.

We must've fallen asleep at the same time, because, when Shannon finally returned to the room, it felt like I'd had one of those falling dreams where I woke up before hitting the ground. As I heard his voice, my face touched the ground, and I startled awake. The sound of his voice pierced my ears.

Then he *tsked* me. "You've been a very naughty girl, Blaire."

I just stared at him.

"She isn't Mason's daughter."

I swallowed the lump in my throat.

Scout sat upright, paying attention now.

"Does she know?"

I nodded; she knew Mason wasn't her biological father, but he had raised her as his own.

"Who is the father?"

I gave him my best blank face.

"Let me have a peak then." Shannon placed the folder onto the table near the gurney, and his long fingers curled around my ankle, sending a jolt of electricity, then the pain moved up my leg.

I tried kicking him off me, but he had an iron grip.

His eyes rolled into the back of his head, his mouth parted, and then he trembled.

If what I thought was correct, then Shannon could see my memories by touching me, like what he had done at the nightclub by showing me a memory and very similar to what a clairvoyant could do. The more I got to know Shannon, the more I realized he was like an onion; apart from making me cry, he had layers. Each layer of his psyche held a different flavor of monster. He was a vampire first, his anger made him shift into a creature with devil horns, and he held elements akin to a clairvoyant. He was definitely dabbling in his own medicine in order to have so many different powers. What I knew about this gift, it only worked if I thought about that memory or what the person looked like. I didn't want Shannon to know Scout's true father's identity. Nobody knew. Not even Old Man, aka Salvador. Shannon might know the flavor of creature he was, but he didn't have to know the true man behind the monster.

Shannon dug around my subconscious, searching for what he wanted.

I thought about flowers in spring, *zap*, a bee making honey, *zap*, glancing up at a tree, *zap*, then a shadowy figure appeared. No, I could not think of *him*. The figure looked like a hologram, but luckily, his features weren't clear. I had to move my thoughts from *him* and thought of the beach, *zap*. The pain Shannon caused every time I tried to shift my thoughts from *him* was like a swarm of bees stinging my ankle repeatedly on the same spot. I wouldn't last if he carried on like this. Shannon was too powerful.

I did what I was taught and reached to touch Shannon. I would use what was at my disposal. Visions of Ma came into focus, *zap*. I absorbed that electric shock and pushed it through my hand and into the arm I was holding. *Zap*. Again, I absorbed the shock and shoved it into Shannon without thinking about it.

The mystery figure started to appear. Again, he remained in shadows, but his eyes glowed blue.

Shannon was busy breaking down my resistance, crushing my walls until he found the image he was looking for.

If I wanted Shannon to stop touching and zapping me,

I had to do something hard and fast. It would have to be something that sent him away from me and pretty quickly. I dug in my treasure chest filled with powerful goodies I'd been hoarding for years. Finally, I could use this gift bestowed upon me. I would wait for the right time before I passed this one to Shannon.

A vision of Scout in my arms as a newborn baby, *zap*, and I shoved that shock, along with the lightning bolt from my treasure chest, and sent it into Shannon. The instant the shock and the bolt left me, it threw Shannon against the far wall, with the smell of singed hair assaulting my nose.

Shannon hit it with a loud thud and laughed.

His Soldier Boys, in shock from what I had done, immediately pointed their weapons at me.

I smiled as I stared at him. Now that Shannon was no longer gripping my foot, the burning sensation left me, leaving a cold rush in its wake.

"If the glimpse of the image I saw was real, it's amazing he didn't kill you. He is powerful," Shannon said between deep breaths. The impact of hitting the wall had only momentarily stung him.

I groaned, and my smile morphed into a tight line. This was not how I wanted Scout to learn the truth. My blank stare resumed; I wouldn't answer any of his questions. The less he knew, the better. Even though he might know who the man was, he didn't have to know any of the details.

"Love would've been his ultimate weakness, so I understand why he had to leave you. But you didn't tell him he had a child. If you did, I could only assume he would've taken her with him. Your secret is safe with me. It's not my secret to tell. But that would explain Scout's talent, would it not?"

Salvation

I turned to Scout, and she blinked wide eyes at me, shell shocked.

"Tell me, Blaire, what other talents does Scout have? She is a necromancer, obviously. Please tell, what else can she do?"

I bit my lip. I didn't trust my voice at that moment.

"Blaire?" That one word sent shivers down my spine. "Tell me, or I may have to tell your secret."

It wasn't exactly a fair question, as both answers were potentially dangerous for Scout—to let Shannon know all she could do or let Scout find out who her real father was. Would it be so bad if she knew? Yes, it would be. It was one of the weakest moments in my life—*love*, the truest kind. Without it, I would never have had Scout. I had loved him, but he had left me. Our relationship was doomed from the start, and he wasn't exactly meant for this world. And yes, if I had told him I was pregnant, he might have stayed but at the risk of losing everything. His family would have kicked him out.

Then an idea came to me—perhaps if Scout *showed* Shannon what she could do. My smile returned. "What would you say if Scout did a little demonstration?"

"I don't think so." Shannon shook his head.

Okay, so he wasn't gullible.

"What about one of your soldiers?"

"Fine." He waved at the closest soldier.

I turned to Scout and placed her hands in mine. "Remember what I told you not to do?"

She nodded hesitantly.

"Well, forget what I said, and do that which changes them first, and then do the other one," I said with a wicked wink.

We climbed off the gurney, and she approached the soldier Shannon had pointed out, the closest one to us.

Scout touched his forearm and closed her eyes. "Bring him a mirror." She opened her eyes.

Another soldier lifted a handheld mirror to the soldier Scout was holding, and he screamed.

Shannon came to his soldier's aid and lifted the mirror so he could see.

His soldier had aged prematurely. But that was only in the mirror and only when Scout was touching him.

Shannon burst out laughing. "Nice party trick."

Scout released the soldier's arm.

He looked in the mirror again to see his youthful features staring back at him. His shoulders sagged with relief.

Huh, who would've thought that the soldiers were a little vain?

"What else?" Shannon now stood beside Scout.

Perhaps this was the moment I had been waiting for. The boys might be on their way to rescue us, but right now, I needed to get Scout away from Shannon. If she used her gift on him and I killed as many Soldier Boys as I could and freed Mason from the panic room, then the three of us should be able to escape. We could use the soldiers' guns against them. It could be easy enough. Crossing fingers, it would work.

When Shannon moved, we had him right where we wanted him.

I yelled, "Now!" and a few things happened at once. Scout bulldozed into Shannon, both her palms hitting his chest as hard as she could. The impact jettisoned Shannon's soul from his body, and he flew through the walls and out the room.

Before Soldier Boy could react, I grabbed his firearm and blasted a hole into his chest, obliterating his heart, his body crumpling to the ground. Next, I fired at the Soldier Boy who had charged at us. The bullet hit his head, and his brains burst out the back and onto the wall behind him. Two more soldiers ran in the room. In two quick successions, I fired at each of their heads, killing them instantly.

Before I could obliterate Shannon's body, it collapsed to the floor when his soul flew back into the room. He took one look at his body lying on the ground, glared at me with murderous intent and slipped back into his body.

Scout and I froze as we watched Shannon's body reanimate. Slowly, he rose. I pushed Scout behind me as we distanced ourselves from him. My hand trembled as I squeezed the gun handle.

"I see why you needed to hide her," Shannon drawled. One side of his face had lost its muscle as his eye drooped, revealing more white than pupil and iris. One side of his lip hung, and his arm lay limp at his side. Somehow, with the impact of his body hitting the floor and his soul reanimating him, he didn't realign himself.

I didn't understand it. Scout had only done it once before and with a dog. Unfortunately, the dog had died.

Scout screamed when Shannon lunged at us.

His good hand grabbed my hair, bunching it in his fist as he pulled.

I screamed, "Run, Scout! Run, baby! Don't look back."

Scout ran around us, trying to flee.

Shannon screeched, the ear-piercing sound echoing within the walls. "No! Stay here if you want your mother to live, Scout."

"Don't listen to him!" I cried out, grabbing hold of Shannon's hand as he pulled my hair. With my fingers touching his skin, he pushed power into me, and my world rippled. He shoved memories of my mother into me with such force it knocked the wind out of me.

Flashes of Ma flew at me from all sides—him inserting something inside her, injecting her with stuff I couldn't see, growth of a baby on a monitor. Then slides of Salvador, he wore clothes from another century. He fought battles on horses, using his power to obliterate humans in his way. He, Alex, and Shannon rode together, moving from one town to the next, draining one human until the last.

In the distance, I heard Scout screaming, and I fought my way to get to her. I clawed at anything in front of me until I found soft tissue. I dug my fingers into that tender flesh until Shannon released me. Somehow, I had dug my fingernail into his good eye.

He was cradling it, screeching like a banshee.

"Do it again, Scout," I called out to her.

It was now or never. If Shannon grabbed hold of either me or Scout, I wasn't sure what he would do with us. Even though he had only shown me images, flashes of lives once lived, what would he show me next? Pain, sorrow, death? I didn't want to stick around for that.

With Shannon no longer holding me and blinding me, I could see.

Scout ran toward Shannon. As she was about to touch him, he shoved her away. That instant of her touching him, his soul moved an inch from his body then returned.

Squeezing the gun, I knew I had one round left. I raised it to meet his head as he turned around. My eyes met his as his widened. I fired, hitting him in the face.

"Do it again, Scout. Hit him again."

Scout obeyed and hit Shannon's chest with all her strength.

Shannon's soul flung from his body as it dropped to the floor.

I grabbed the solder's firearm who I had hit in the head and shot Shannon full of holes until it clicked empty.

"Enough, Mom!"

I snapped from my zone. As I glanced at Shannon's body, his soul bellowed in a fiery rage, but it was too late. We had destroyed his body. A vessel no longer existed for him to return to.

Through my exhaustion, I whistled and called upon the ferryman to collect Shannon's soul.

The man in his boat floated past us, whistling the same tune, and Shannon's soul followed him whether he wanted to or not.

Shannon's soul glanced at me, grimaced in pain or hate —I wasn't sure and didn't care—then reluctantly went with the ferryman.

None of the Soldier Boy's souls joined Shannon, and I suspected they didn't have any. He had grown them in a lab, and they were not natural monsters.

The ferryman waved at me and carried on down the river of souls. His eyes spied me out the back of his head. Yeah, it was creepy, but the ferryman had eyes there. Go figure.

I turned to Scout on the floor who was shaking like a leaf. I crouched and wrapped my arms around her. "You did well, my sweetheart. It was perfect."

I heard her swallow.

"Did I just see that? His soul and a ferryman?" she asked hoarsely.

I smiled and nodded motherly. "Yes. The ferryman owes me a couple favors. When called, he fetches the souls who need delivering to the underworld." I kissed the top of her head and helped her to stand. "Are you okay?"

"Uh-huh." Her voice quivered.

I brought her in for a hug and embraced the crap out of her. I kissed her gently on her forehead, temple, and head, ensuring everything was still there and intact, with tears streaking my face. That was my baby girl's first monster fight, and she did so well. She was scary as hell and a threat to every single monster out there in the big, bad world. But I would be there for her every step of the way.

"You were awesome, Scout. It's scary what you can do, but, by god, we needed you to do it. Shannon would not stop if we didn't do something first."

"But he was your father."

"No." I shook my head. "He wasn't. He just stuck his sperm in a tube and fertilized my mother's egg, and whatever else he injected her with to create me. He was an abomination, along with his soldiers. I hope that's all of them now." I scanned to ensure those on the floor were in fact dead and listened for any footsteps heading our way.

"What about the other vampire?"

"What other vampire?"

"There's another one around here."

My brows furrowed in confusion. I knew we had killed Noryx when we rescued Sebastian. I hadn't seen Raphael, but he wasn't a vampire. So, I wasn't sure who she meant. And I didn't see another vampire when I had first arrived here. He must be hiding from us.

"I didn't see him when I got here. But, if he's still around here, we'll get to him when he shows himself."

Looking up at me, she asked with her big green puppy-dog eyes, "Who is my father? My *real* father."

Salvation

I sighed. Pain shot into my shoulder now that my adrenaline was tapering off. Closing my eyes, I sucked in a breath.

Now, for the moment of truth.

Chapter Thirty

"I can't tell you much, but what I can say is he loved me with all his heart. But our love was forbidden and doomed to begin with. It was a huge risk for him to even see me. And, yes, if he had known about you, he would have taken you from me."

She frowned; frustration written on her face. "Why?"

"I can't tell you any more than that, Scout. I'm sorry. I can't say anymore." What I didn't say was that by just us mentioning him might summon him.

Her eyes widened as she thought of something. "Is he a daemon?"

I burst out laughing. "No!" I cringed at how close she was at guessing.

Her hands were on her hips, and she was staring at me like she would at Christmas time when she wanted to know what presents were under the tree.

I embraced her again. "I'm serious, Scout, I can't tell you anymore. Or he'll know we're talking about him, and then he'll discover you and will want to take you back with him. I can't have that." Just thinking about him could be like a nudge in his direction; I even had to stop thinking about him.

Footsteps sounded quickly in our direction; we stopped talking as we listened. I grabbed the nearest gun and pointed it at the door. The person stopped running and was now walking closer. The door handle turned slowly. My finger was on the trigger, and I squeezed it just a little without firing.

I saw the blond hair first and lowered my shaking arm. I ran to Sebastian, wrapping my limbs around his body. "You found us."

"The GPS tracker is still in your earrings."

I lifted my head off his shoulder to stare at the man I was in love with and kissed him as passionately as possible.

"Eww, gross. Get a room," Scout said behind us.

Sebastian and I laughed, and I climbed off his body.

"Let's get Mason." I approached the large vault, punched in the number I had seen them use and tugged on the door.

As it swung open, blasts of hot air blustered behind us.

We all turned to see a Noryx's lookalike clone staring at us. It was unnerving, considering we had killed the original at the mountains.

The man had identical features to Noryx but was shorter and his hair was a shade darker. He eyed his master's body and scowled, obviously unhappy we had killed Shannon. "Which of you killed my brother? And my master?"

Mason exited the vault, and the four of us watched the Noryx twin, unsure what he would do, considering we had killed his brother and now his master.

"I guess it's just one of those things. You take one of

ours, we take one of yours," I replied nonchalantly, adding a shrug for added emphasis.

Before any of us could react, the Noryx twin screeched and charged us.

Mason pushed Scout toward me—a protective fatherly move—and lunged at the vampire.

Sebastian tried to push Mason out of the way, but the Noryx twin already had Mason in his vise grip, and they both collapsed to the floor. Neither of them moved, then the vampire turned into a cloud of ash—dirtying the floor.

We ran to Mason, who was clutching a blade to his chest. I hadn't seen the vampire hold anything when he charged for us, yet a weapon was sticking out of Mason.

"He was a tricky vampire," Mason said, coughing up blood. "What I did to him was mirrored onto me."

I stood, shaking my head. "What do you mean?"

"I grabbed the blade off the table and used it on the vampire." Mason pointed to the blade sticking from his chest. "The moment I stuck it into his heart, it ricocheted and pierced me. Whoever killed the vampire ultimately killed himself in the process too."

"No, no, no, no, no!" I cried out.

Scout was beside me, crying.

"Let me try and help you."

"No, Blaire. You can't mend this." Mason paled and closed his eyes as his breathing came in slow and shallow.

"You have to let me try." I cried, ignoring Mason's pleas to stop me. Holding his hand in mine, I lowered my shields. I summoned my white light and pushed it into Mason's cold hand. I went to his heart first, and all I found was goodness. He was the man who had loved me from the moment we had met and had adopted Scout as his own. He was an angel sent to protect us, to protect Scout.

Salvation

The blade was stuck in his heart, and his beat was slowing.

I frantically searched for his flicker of life. When I found it, his light was barely there. I picked it up and tried to reignite it. But it wasn't working.

Slowly, his flame became smaller and smaller, until it winked out.

And I was in his darkness and scared. I heard Scout's cries, and it pained me to know Mason wouldn't be there for her anymore. He was her father—the best any child could want. Slowly, my aura moved from his body into mine, where I tightly shut my shields and opened my eyes.

Scout was crying on top of Mason's chest, my own tears flowed, and Sebastian sat beside me with a hand on my shoulder for comfort. My body moved mechanically, on autopilot, while my heart hammered in my chest, replaying what had happened, finding no council in any scenario.

Either way, whoever had killed the vampire would have ended up dead.

Chapter Thirty-One

Léon had ensured Scout had a room by the time we arrived at the Labyrinth. Two guards watched over her while she slept. It was overkill, but she was mine, and I wanted her safe. She had just helped in killing Shannon, lost a parent, and was understandably exhausted—physically and emotionally.

The sun was rising by the time we all settled down, and Léon kissed me goodbye before retiring for the day. I would see him after 4 p.m., which was his usual wake-up time. Even though it was still light at 4 p.m., he didn't have to sleep until nightfall; he was powerful enough to wake just before. Hence, the Labyrinth had no windows to let in sunlight.

Construction workers were already on site to fix the large gaping hole in the nightclub, but apparently, Léon wanted to turn it into a spa for vampires.

I had laughed at the idea, but he was dead serious.

He was busy renovating a warehouse where he would move the nightclub; it was much larger and with ample parking. Not only that, nobody would try their luck to enter the Labyrinth.

I lay in Sebastian's arms, our naked bodies pressed against one another's, and our chests were heaving. I wiped beads of sweat off my forehead and sat up on my right elbow to give Sebastian my attention. We were discussing our current situation now that there were three of us.

"I love you both, and I don't know how we'll do this," I admitted sadly.

He chuckled then grinned. "Yeah, babe, I don't know either. But Léon has shared before—"

"Oh?" Now I was intrigued.

"Maybe it's not for me to say."

"No, please tell me. You have to now. You can't raise this topic without giving me the details."

"Léon has only loved one other that I know of, and he shared her with Jean-René."

I groaned. Recalling my last interaction with Jean-René sent a shiver up my spine, and it had not been pleasurable. I guess that's why Jean-René had behaved that way toward me; he loved Léon and not just in a best-friend kind of way. He was protecting his friend ... from me.

"But they aren't together now?"

"No." He grinned. "Now they're just the best of friends who'll do anything to keep the other out of harm's way." He pulled me closer. "It's not my story to tell, Blaire."

My lips touched his, begging him to speak. When I came back up for air, he chuckled.

"You're so evil." He winked, smacking my naked ass. "Fine, but if Léon ever asks, you didn't hear it from me."

"Sure, fine. I won't say anything. Now tell me."

"She was human and fell in love with both of them. She was their world, the kindest person you would have ever met, with a heart of gold." His fingers lightly caressed my back. "Disaster struck when another vampire bit her. Till this day, they don't know who it was. Léon suspected it was an old jealous lover of his. Anyway, she was turned into a vampire, and it changed her in more ways than the obvious. She went from being kind and precious to sad and despairing. Her new power dampened their relationship so much they were basically forced to give her up. She was mean and calculating to put the cherry on top. So, I don't think they were missing much. They buried their love for her and moved on. And I don't think either of them have had someone they truly loved ever again." He stopped caressing, and his stare bore a hole through my face that made me want to squirm away. "Until now …" He caressed my shoulder again. "And I suspect Jean-René is jealous of you for catching Léon's eye."

"It wasn't on purpose."

"I know, Léon knows too, but Jean-René is a vindictive asshole. But my brother will protect you from Jean-René's assholery." He chuckled, and it sent goosebumps all over my body—the good kind.

I lay my head on his chest with my left arm draped over his abdomen and allowed his heartbeat to calm my nerves. I breathed in sync with him.

"I love you," I said and kissed his chest then looked up at him.

I melted in his smile as he pulled me closer to his face and kissed me with the fiery passion I would never grow tired of.

Part III

TWO YEARS LATER

Chapter Thirty-Two

Sebastian thumbed my bottom lip, cupped my face, and planted a delicious kiss on my lips before heading to the leap. I sipped on my decaf and waited.

Scout finally left the bathroom, wearing all black. It was the typical attire for teenagers who were busy going through the various stages of their early lives—the teenage years.

"Is that what you're wearing? I guess it makes sense. If we need to go to a funeral afterward, you won't have to change."

"Even you're wearing black." She pointed at my shirt.

"It's a navy-blue shirt with blue jeans. You know you're allowed to wear clothes with colors. In fact, I insist on it. It's dark out. What if we can't see you?"

"I'm wearing this." She pouted and folded her arms.

"Fine, but are you ready, or do you still need to powder your nose?" I winked wickedly at her and rose from my chair, taking one last sip of my coffee.

"I'm done. We can go." Her hands moved to her hips, and her foot tapped anxiously.

"Come, sweet cheeks. Let's pop that cherry."

She grunted, rolling her eyes.

Ralph was blaring his horn by the time I locked the front door.

Scout waved and ran to him.

Devan sat in the front seat, so the two of us climbed into the back.

"Are you ladies ready?" Ralph chimed, his eyes on Scout, sharing a proud moment with her.

Scout beamed at him, her head bobbing in excitement, hands clapping.

We headed to the only cemetery in town. It was smack in the middle of Sterling Meadow, and something was living there that shouldn't be. Slayerbody had hired us, the anonymous organization who usually sent us our assignments. We didn't know what flavor monster we were up against, just that we should kill it before law enforcement learned about it or it harmed someone—again.

I squeezed Scout to my body while she tried to pry herself away from me, groaning. The almost-sixteen-year-old hated my hugs; they were gross and unnecessary. I thought otherwise, stealing hugs and kisses regularly.

"Are you sure you're ready?" I asked for the umpteenth time.

She rolled her eyes. "Yes ..." She drawled out the word in frustration and bratty teenager-ism. She had been ready for months, but this would be her first *official* assignment.

"Good." I pulled her in for another hug.

She finally relinquished, wrapping her arms around my waist and hugging me back. Her affection was most welcomed.

I let her go and stared ahead, meeting her excited gaze. Yep, she had grown considerably and was now taller than me. It was official; I was now the shortest person in our entire extended family.

She turned on her heel and approached Ralph, who was waiting patiently for her. They would be teaming up tonight, while Devan and I hung back—for when they needed us.

I exhaled a shaky breath yet beamed with pride. I giggled when I saw Ralph remove a yellow manila folder to review the plan with her. Ralph was painfully organized, but it's what the team needed. We all brought our various flavor of strengths to Ulysses, and now that Ralph knew all about my powers and Scout's, we were stronger for it.

For a moment, I wondered what Marcus was up to but didn't wonder for too long, didn't care. We hadn't seen or spoken to him in over two years. But Troy informed me they were staying out of trouble, living the quiet life on a ranch somewhere. I was glad for them; he and Melanie had accepted their beast and had moved past their trouble and now lived a happy life together.

The wind stopped blowing, and the insects went quiet.

I flinched as if something had burned my back. I spun to see what was behind me. My eyes locked on him, jaw slack.

Time stood still, literally, except for us.

My skin pebbled at the sight of him. The air was sucked from my lungs until it stung. I collapsed to my knees, right where he wanted me, where he needed me.

His towering stature stood spine chillingly in front of me.

I sat on my haunches, staring up at the dark figure looming over me, his power thrumming against my chest like drums.

"Blaire ..." His voice was deep, thunderous, and bloodcurdling. He extended a hand.

I couldn't hesitate taking it. I dared not to insult him. When I finally found my voice, I said one word, "Vic," and swallowed hard, the back of my throat hurting, threatening tears. I rose to my feet, my hand still in his.

His meaty fingers enveloped mine with the threat of pain edging near. "It's been a while." His fiery gaze met mine.

All I managed was a nod then averted my gaze to my feet.

"Look at me, Blaire," he commanded, his voice tight with stoic calm.

I had to obey. Glancing up again, I met his now tender, smiling eyes.

He smirked. "Sorry I haven't called."

My heart hammered in my chest. My stomach was now firmly at my feet. Wind blew from behind him, forcing me to step backward, so I didn't fall over. A glaze of film encircled us, separating us from the world. Time was unfrozen, and I heard yelling behind me. "You left me." I finally said.

He glanced over my head at the action behind me and nodded. "I had to." His hand that was holding mine pulsed with heat. "I had no choice. You know how the family can be." His smile was warm, comforting, but sadness filled his eyes. His face was a whirlwind of emotions left unsaid over years of absenteeism. "You didn't tell me ..." He jerked his chiseled chin in Scout's direction.

"You left me," I repeated, shaking my head in defeat. "You didn't even leave a note." My voice quivered with buried emotions now bubbling to the surface, like a tsunami. "How could I tell you?"

"I know." He watched her.

I turned to see her slam her palms into the creature; they had stitched together various body parts, creating a man with two heads, four arms, two legs, and a torso double the width of a strong man. Two ghouls flew from the creature after Scout's palms slammed into the creature's chest.

Ralph severed two of its arms with a scythe.

It spun from the momentum and was about to fall on top of him when Scout unsheathed her blade to decapitate one of the heads. The body crashed to the ground, blood splattering all over them and pooling where it lay.

Ralph sliced the body again, removing the other head.

The two ghouls howled, realizing their host was now a lump of dead meat. They retreated into a nearby crypt.

Scout and Ralph high-fived each other, blood splashing on her face.

My excitement was short lived when I turned to face Vic.

His wings extended, spreading behind him in all their splendor. "She has to come with me." His voice was calm, his power gently thrumming.

My nerve crumpled at my feet, along with all sense of feeling. "You don't have to do this, Vic. Please." Dropping to my knees again, I reached for his feet to grovel.

"She wields my powers. It's not safe for her here. She needs to be with me."

I knew he was right, but I couldn't lose her again.

"Stand, Blaire." He reached for my hand and pulled me to my feet again, glancing at my abdomen. "I'll let her visit when the little one arrives." He smiled, his eyes gleaming in the evening light.

I rubbed my stomach. "Five months along."

"Congratulations. I see it's a boy this time."

"Yes. We're still deciding on a name."

"Is it the leopard's or the vampire's?"

I ignored his question, because I knew he knew who the father was.

When Scout shouted behind me, I glanced over my shoulder, bursting with pride at how she had handled herself with her first monster, but I couldn't enjoy the festivities now. Not yet.

"Please don't take her away from me, Vic. Or at least let her choose."

He pursed his lips, narrowing his eyes. "For her to choose, she needs to see my world." He considered my request then grunted. "I'll allow you time to say goodbye and will return to collect her in three days." He brought me in for an embrace then abruptly let go.

As he flapped his wings, they changed from white to a silver shine then a purple hue, and then he disappeared in the blink of an eye. The film that had cocooned us popped the moment Vic left.

My hands gripped my stomach out of instinct to protect the little guy. I turned in time to watch Scout and Ralph fist-bump Devan, then they headed in my direction. A cold sweat hit me like a frigid shower, the lump in my throat harder to swallow.

I watched them approach with my eyes wide and a cottonmouth.

There was no easy way to tell Scout her real father was about to take her away from me in three days' time. But that maybe she could return, if she wanted. His family would not allow her to leave.

And to make it worse, he was the angel of death—the deity who controlled the dead.

Next in the Blaire Thorne Series

vinci-books.com/underworld-legacy

Secrets, danger, and an unknown future await.

Scout finally meets her father, the Lord of the Underworld, while I'm pregnant and everything is about to shatter. A normal son in a world of monsters—how does he fit in? As the truth unravels, I fear what happens if our baby never changes.

Turn the page for a free preview…

Underworld Legacy: Chapter One

Léon climbed onto the bed and pulled me into the curve of his warm, naked body. Usually, he'd be cool to the touch, but whenever we were together, he ensured warmth. He'd just fed on one of his many tasty treats who lived at the Labyrinth, but that's where it ended. He'd said he only wanted me even though he shared me with Sebastian, although never in the same bed.

He kissed my temple, then my cheek and down my neck. With one delicate caress of his fingertips, my body hummed for more attention. When he stopped, I moaned my frustration.

"You know what the doctor said."

I frowned and turned my angry glare at him. "Just that I had to be careful," I said and pouted.

"And we are. You already have one scar." He trailed a finger over my swollen belly and traced along the scar that ran from bellybutton down to my pelvic area. I had more scars, but he wasn't referring to those. Now that I had my memory back, I remembered that awful day when Scout was born. She had been in respiratory distress and they had to get her out immediately. The umbilical cord had wrapped around her neck, and if the doctor didn't get her out in those few minutes, she would've met her dad in one of the worst ways possible. It was a blessing she'd survived and one I wouldn't forget.

I groaned again. "You sound like Sebastian."

"As I should. We only want what's best for you and our son."

I folded my arms across my breasts, but they were so engorged I couldn't keep my hands there, so I rested them on my stomach instead.

The little guy kicked, and I gasped.

"He heard you." I grabbed Léon's hand and placed it against the side where the baby had just kicked. The little one was using my insides for soccer practice, but it made my men happy to feel him move around.

"I can't wait to meet him." Léon's smile reached his dark blue eyes as he considered me and caressed my side. "He's our miracle."

Tears filled my eyes.

We knew how it happened but didn't think it was possible, and would never question it. It was another gift from the Gods I'd gladly take. Léon and Sebastian were old and powerful hunters of the night. We never suspected either could make a child, so we never used protection. Me falling pregnant had never crossed our minds.

When I blinked, the waterworks started, and Léon kissed away my tears.

"I hope they're tears of joy. You know I hate it when you sad-cry." He pouted and gave me puppy-dog eyes. His expression was so endearing and strange all at once, because his facade was usually one of control and dominance.

I snorted, wiping away the remaining wetness from my cheek. "They are. I'm just emotional lately. And... I'm worried about you, Sebastian, Scout, and now this little fella." I rubbed my stomach.

"Ah, Scout. Have you told her yet?"

I shook my head.

"You need to tell her. The longer you leave it, the worse it will be for both of you. What happens if you only tell her the moment she's meant to leave."

"I only found out yesterday. I'm trying to decide the best way to tell her, but I know. I will speak with her today. She's coming with us on another case."

"Good, spend time with her before she goes. You only have two days left."

I nodded, and more tears flowed.

Léon tsked me. "I need to get your mind off everything making you sad." Before I could reply, he was between my legs with his magical tongue and powerful fingers. With one hand caressing a breast, he sent his velvety power into me and gave me what I needed... a small release to take the edge off that wouldn't endanger the baby.

Grab your copy...
vinci-books.com/underworld-legacy

About the Author

A Multi-genre author writing twisted endings...

N Gray is a USA Today Bestselling Author who lives in Cape Town, South Africa, with her daughter and adopted cat named Miss Beans.

During the day, she's an analyst and provider profiler for a medical insurance company. At night, she types on her curved keyboard, creating fictional characters some may love and others you want to kill yourself.

She writes in four genres: urban fantasy, thriller, horror, and paranormal romance.

She now writes under Natalie Michaels for her new thrillers and SD Syns for her new horrors.

Acknowledgments

Thank you to my readers, old and new, for taking a chance on my books.

You are the reason I write the stories I do. As long as you keep reading, I'll keep writing.

I'm truly humbled by your support and encouragement.

I write in as many genres as I love reading in. There are so many stories swarming inside my head that I could never just choose one.

Horror is my guilty pleasure. I love writing short stories filled with dark humour and the occult with a twist ending.

Urban fantasy and paranormal romance are where I love to spend my time, and I have so many books planned that I don't have enough time (*but I'll get there*).

And lastly, my thrillers. Who doesn't love sitting on the edge of their seat while reading about what goes on inside the antagonist's mind? Well, I love writing about them.

www.ingramcontent.com/pod-product-compliance
Ingram Content Group UK Ltd.
Pitfield, Milton Keynes, MK11 3LW, UK
UKHW040247291225
466476UK00003B/18